The Ascent of Faith

The Ascent of
Faith

John Highhouse

To my Church,
May you seek to know Christ

Contents

The Call

Prayerful stood in stunned silence as he watched the messenger exit his home, his heart pounding in excitement over what he had just been told. *Could it really be?* He had not been prepared for such a message and was not quite sure what he should do. After a few moments of stunned silence, he began excitedly pacing back and forth in front of the small, warm fireplace while his mind was trying to recover from the shock of the man's words.

In a matter of minutes, restlessness overtook him. He walked over to the door, put on his cloak, and went outside, hoping that the cool spring air and the clear, star-filled sky would help him sort out his thoughts. The full moon allowed him to glance around and see the forms of the nearby homes. He longed to run to the nearest house to tell his friends about his visitor; however, he needed some time alone first.

Trudging around the back of his own house, Prayerful walked along on the soft grass and easily found the trail leading to his favorite spot where he would often sit and meditate. In a few minutes, he climbed a hill overlooking the serene valley cradling the nearby river. Making his way over to the large rock resting under an ancient oak, he noticed the melody of the spring peepers and was thankful for this peaceful place, especially on a night like this.

Sitting down on the large boulder, he gazed into the distance across the River of Death to where he knew the Celestial City stood. He had always loved to read his Bible and pray at this spot, especially since, on very clear days, he could catch a tiny glimpse of that magnificent place across the river. Prayerful let his eyes shift to the valley below and gazed at the few houses on this side of the river, noticing the soft glow of candlelight coming from a few of the windows. Some of his closest friends he had ever known lived in those homes, but the message he just received made him think of his closest friend ever: Believer.

It seemed like yesterday when he had met this man at Palace Beautiful after they each had just begun their own pilgrimage. The bond of friendship had been immediate as they shared their stories of how they had come to the cross. Prayerful remembered being quite excited when they had decided to join each other's company even though neither one of them had any idea what challenges and dangers they were about to face.

Prayerful cherished the memories of how they had helped each other through many difficult days and had even drawn their swords together in defense of the truth. He would never forget their morning sword practice and often grieved with his friend over the fact that Believer's twin brother, Pretender, refused to follow the King. Truly, throughout their journey, Believer and Prayerful had grown as brothers.

It had been a difficult time for Prayerful when, after finishing their pilgrimage, the King sent his messenger for Believer.   Prayerful still clearly remembered when Believer spoke to him, saying that the King of the Celestial City had sent for him — it was his time to cross the River of Death and enter the Celestial City. A tear slipped down Prayerful's cheek as he thought about the last time he saw his old friend. He still missed him.

As Prayerful was reflecting on their adventures, the memory of another man could not be forgotten — Passionate for Truth. Believer spoke very highly of this warrior of faith, and Prayerful eventually learned how this man had not only helped countless Pilgrims on their way to the Celestial City, but also how he lead the charge in many battles for the King. Passionate for Truth was a zealous man with unwavering commitment to God.

Prayerful was grateful that he was able to meet this soldier before the King called Passionate across the river. He still could clearly remember the challenge that Passionate gave before he left. While standing on the riverbank, this veteran of many battles handed his sword to Believer and said, "I have carried the sword of my father and my grandfather for many years now. It is the sword of one who is zealous for truth.   It is the sword of one who will never compromise. Who will bear it now? As my father left his sword to the one who would pick it up after him and bring it forth into battle for the King, so do I. This is not a weapon for cowards, nor is it a weapon for compromisers. Who will carry it? … Most of all, who will give his life, his all, for the One who purchased his salvation?"

Prayerful remembered how he and Believer were greatly moved by this challenge. They often talked about it over the next several days while they kept Passionate's weapon. They did not know who would eventually take up the call to bear the sword, but they wanted to be ready to give it to whomever the King would choose. As time passed, however, no one came, and the sword remained idle. Even after Believer crossed the river, Prayerful continued to hold onto the precious weapon while he and their other traveling companions, Temperance and Gentleness, waited for the King to call them.

Other changes took place in the months that followed Believer's crossing. A godly man named Steadfast came along, and soon he and Gentleness were married. This wonderful couple was a big encouragement to Prayerful, for their love for the Lord overflowed into every area of life. They rented a house near Gentleness's mother, Temperance, and would often invite Prayerful over for a meal and fellowship.

As more pilgrims came from their journey to this valley, Prayerful was saddened by the fact that it seemed that Steadfast was one of the only ones who genuinely had a focus on God. There were many who had bags full of goods from Vanity Fair, and Prayerful watched as every one of these bags was lost in the river while the person was crossing to the Celestial City. Others who came to the River of Death seemed quite groggy from the Enchanted Grounds, having their spiritual senses lulled to sleep. Prayerful wondered how they could make it across the river, and each time he wanted to shout, "Awake, awake; put on thy strength! ... It is high time to awake out of sleep!" Despite his reservations, however, such Pilgrims somehow made it across. It was as if the river itself helped wake them up, but by then, it was too late for them to accomplish anything for the Lord — their lives had been wasted.

Prayerful's heart was continually burdened, for

many of these Pilgrims loved to converse about the things of the world but few talked about the things of God. Those who did speak of their King usually came from the village of False Piety, for, even though they worshipped the Lord with their mouth, their lives were spent on the things of Vanity. Such people would talk abundantly of their love for their Savior, yet the slightest inconvenience would keep them from church. They would speak of being a witness, yet they rarely followed Christ in simple areas of obedience. Their actions were continually displaying a life that contradicted their words.

Prayerful's heart grew more and more troubled as he witnessed so many Pilgrims who seemed to lack a genuine love for God. At times his burdened heart would overflow in the form of tears. Prayerful never grew calloused to seeing such apathy in others, but rather, he grew even more burdened day by day. As time passed, he began to spend more and more time in prayer about this issue. If he could do nothing else about it, he certainly could pray.

A cool breeze rustled nearby leaves and caused a shiver to go up Prayerful's spine as he sat dwelling upon all of these thoughts. He wrapped his cloak around him a little more as he shifted his mind to reflect on the events of the past few days.

Temperance had been ill for a while, and the King's messenger eventually came for her, announcing that her turn to cross the River of Death had arrived. As Prayerful had stood with Steadfast and Gentleness saying goodby to her, a seed was planted in his heart. Prayerful knew that he had only a limited time on this side of the river, and he wanted to do more for God. There was a great need, especially since so many other Pilgrims were living for the world. This seed of longing grew over the next several weeks, and he knew that he had to do something more in service for the Lord.

Prayerful understood that he was not a great soldier, so he hoped that maybe he could deliver Passionate for Truth's sword to the one who should carry it. Since the days were dark and wicked, someone needed to take a stand in this evil day, doing all they could to stand — but who?

As Prayerful sat on the rock, dwelling upon these things, a thrill of excitement shot through him as he thought: *My prayers were answered tonight!* His heart once again raced with excited joy as he replayed this evening's events through his mind once more. He could hardly believe what had just happened.

Just a few hours ago, he had returned home from talking with Mr. Seeker about they way of the cross. Then, while preparing for bed, the burden of the failure of Pilgrims had fallen upon his heart once again, pulling him to his knees beside the crackling fire. He was there for only a few minutes when he heard the front door of his house squeak open. Startled, he jumped up, looked at the door, and was shocked to see that he was in the presence of one of the King's messengers.

Prayerful did not have time to even think before the man spoke, "The eyes of the LORD are upon the righteous, and his ears are open unto their cry. You are called to find the one who is to bear the sword of Passionate for Truth." Then, just as quickly as the messenger came, he left.

Staring up at the star-filled sky, Prayerful replayed those words over and over in his mind, trying to soak in the reality of this new mission. After a few minutes, Prayerful stood up, his heart almost bursting from excitement, joy, and even fear. He gazed across the valley for one final time as another shiver went up his spine — he had been called.

*   *   *

Prayerful's armor clinked as he moved about his house, collecting what he needed for his journey. Although the exciting message had kept him awake well into the night, he still woke up refreshed and eager to go. He knew that he needed to travel light, thus, he only would bring the essentials. Having been on a long journey with Believer, Prayerful already knew what was most important, and it did not take too long to gather his supplies. Although he did not know how long his search would be, he thought it wise to be prepared for a lengthy journey.

Prayerful gave one final check of his sack, running through his mental checklist. Besides his Bible and certificate of Heavenly Citizenship, the bag also contained his tinder box called the Spark of Spiritual Desire, his lantern of God's Truth, and his small pot and utensils of Daily Devotions. He also brought some bread and his canteen filled with the water of Spiritual Nourishment. All of this was packed together with his Cloak of Resting in God to keep things from banging together.

He slung the leather strap over his head and onto his left shoulder, placing the bag gently on his right side. After his shield found its resting place on his back, Prayerful was finally ready to go. Resting his left hand on the hilt of Passionate's sword hanging at his side, he took one final look around his house, then walked outside, shutting the door. He had just one quick stop to make, and then it would be time to head out into the unknown.

Prayerful made his way to the nearest house

where Steadfast and Gentleness lived. He hated to tell them that he was leaving, especially since they had just said farewell to Temperance, yet he needed to obey the King's call.

Prayerful knocked and was immediately rewarded with an answer as Steadfast opened the door and warmly invited him in. After he entered, Steadfast shut the door behind him, and Prayerful noticed that they were just finishing their morning meal. He was glad that he had caught them while they were both still at home.

"What brings you here so early?" Steadfast questioned.

Prayerful was hoping to break the news in a little more slowly, but such a question drove him to get right to the point. "Well ... I, um ..." he stammered, "I am not really sure how to tell you this, but ... I am leaving on a journey, and I will probably be gone for quite a while."

"What?" Gentleness questioned with her soft voice. "This is so sudden.... Why?"   Both she and Steadfast were clearly stunned.

"A messenger of the King came to my house last night.   I have been called to deliver Passionate for Truth's sword to the next man who is to bear it for the King." Prayerful could see shock written on both of their faces.

"Wow.... That is good news. I know you have been holding onto it for a while now," Steadfast stated after a few moments. "But I am glad that it is going to be passed on to another of the Lord's soldiers." Looking Prayerful in the eyes, he added, "We'll miss you."

"How long will you be gone?" Gentleness asked.

"I don't know.... The messenger never told me who I was to find, and he didn't even tell me where I am to go…. Honestly, I don't know where to begin."

After a few quite moments, Gentleness asked, "Do you think that this person is someone you already know? Maybe it is someone you met on your previous pilgrimage."

"I thought of that as a possibility. The only two men who I think could bear the sword would be Caretaker or Preacher of Truth. I don't think Caretaker is the one simply because he has already been assigned by the King to help Pilgrims who come to Palace Beautiful. Preacher of Truth is certainly a faithful and godly man…. The church that he is pastoring in Vanity clearly shines as a testimony in this dark world; but something tells me that he is not the right one either."

"So, how will you know when you find the right man?" Gentleness asked.

"The Lord will let me know somehow, but I am sure that this man will be one who loves God with all of his heart and his neighbor as himself." After a slight moment he added, "I also expect that he will be skilled with the Sword of the Spirit and will have great discernment and zeal for God."

After another pause, Prayerful felt it necessary to explain a little more. "We have often talked about our observations of various Pilgrims that come to the River of Death…. They are good people — but not godly. Well, I have been praying about this problem for quite a while, hoping that someone would take a stand.

"After Temperance went to the Celestial City several days ago, my heart began to yearn for something more. I cannot sit along the sidelines waiting for my turn to cross the river…. I *need* to do something more. This mission for the King is the answer to both my burden and my prayer. I have been called to serve the Lord… and there is also someone out there who will pick up the sword to fight for the King. Even though my task may not be something big, I consider it an honor that the Lord has counted me faithful, giving me this assignment."

Steadfast gave an understanding nod.

"Although I am not exactly sure where I should go, I do believe that God wants me to head out right away.   This morning while I was praying about it, a verse flew through my mind. 'By faith Abraham, when he was called to go out into a place which he should after receive for an inheritance, obeyed; and he went out, not knowing whither he went.' That is what I need to do as well…. I just wish I knew which way I should go."

After another moment, Steadfast said, "Maybe you should go to Madam Wisdom. She has been around for many years and has studied Scripture more than anyone I know. She might be able to give you some good advice on where to go."

Prayerful's eyes lit up at the suggestion. "That is a good idea!" he declared, as many thoughts began to race through his mind, anticipating the insight she would have. "If there is anyone who can point me in the right direction, she can."

Switching topics, Gentleness asked, "Do you have everything you need?"

"Yes. I only packed the necessities so I can travel light," he replied.   She nodded her head in understanding, but the expression on her face showed that she was not convinced; however, she said nothing more, but instead grew rather pensive.

They talked for a few more minutes until Prayerful declared that he must be on his way. Steadfast then led the group in prayer. Afterward, Prayerful said farewell as he set out to talk with Madam Wisdom.

Madam Wisdom

Prayerful was thankful that the path to Madam Wisdom's house was not very long and that the trail was well-marked. If everything went well, he figured that he would receive good counsel and a direction to travel from Madam Wisdom before the sun reached its peak in the sky.

Trudging along, he breathed deeply of the cool morning air and gazed upward toward the nearly cloudless sky. The smile on his face stretched even wider as he though about the task he had been given. It felt good to be on a journey once again.

Within an hour of travel, he crossed the Stream of Humility and entered the Listening Meadow where many godly men and women would come to pray and meditate. After passing through this grassland, he came to the Hill of the Fear of the Lord.

The slope before him was so steep that it reminded him of the Hill of Difficulty. As he gazed at the hillside before him, he could clearly see why fools and scorners refused to climb it but would rather mock those who struggled to the top, seeking Wisdom. However, Prayerful knew the value of Wisdom was well worth the effort.

He took a deep breath and began working his way up the hill. As Prayerful climbed, his body groaned against the exertion while his heart raced with anticipation of what he might learn.   Progress was tedious, but steady.

Half an hour later, as he crested the top of the hill, he caught his first glance of Wisdom's mansion. Prayerful understood that Wisdom, herself, built the magnificent structure, and he was amazed at its beauty. There was a low stone wall surrounding the residence and a single gate which gave access to the grounds around the great building.   The front porch of the mansion had seven magnificent stone pillars, and the entire building seemed like a beautiful mix between a home and a fortress.

As Prayerful walked down the Path of Knowledge leading to the house, he began to notice rubies, gold, and silver littering the side of the road. He stopped at this sight and cocked his head in confusion for it appeared as if these precious materials had been cast aside like moldy bread.   Within a moment, he noticed a sign nearby that brought clarity to the situation:

> *Wisdom is better than rubies.… How much better*
> *is it to get wisdom than gold! and to get*
> *understanding rather to be chosen than silver!*

Seeing these words, Prayerful subtly nodded his head in understanding. *How truly precious this place must be!*

Continuing on, he soon ascended the seven Steps of Understanding and knocked at the gate of Applied Truth.   Shortly, a servant opened the gate and asked, "How may I help you?"

"My name is Prayerful, and I would like to talk

with Madam Wisdom. I have an important question that she might be able to answer."

"Follow me," the servant replied.

Prayerful entered through the gate and was led across the lawn and around the side of the mansion into a garden full of the Flowers of Good Character. In the midst of the garden, Prayerful beheld a well with a sign above it that read: "Drink of the deep wellspring of Spiritual Knowledge." A white-haired woman stood by the well with a bucket of freshly drawn water. *This must be Madam Wisdom*, Prayerful figured.

The servant brought Prayerful to her and made introductions. "Let me get you something to drink and then we can sit over there to talk," she said, pointing to a nearby flowering tree that shadowed a beautifully carved stone bench.

Prayerful walked over and took a seat while Wisdom poured some water into a cup that she had with her. Soon, she joined him and handed him the cup of the cool, refreshing liquid. After taking a couple swallows, Prayerful briefly told her the story of his pilgrimage with Believer, specifically detailing the account of Passionate for Truth and his sword. He then described how the King's messenger had come to him, and he explained to her the assignment that he had just been given. "And I suppose that leads me to my question for you," he continued. "Since I was never told who would be the recipient of the sword, I am not sure where to look. I was wondering if you would have any suggestions?"

"Have you prayed and examined Scripture?" Wisdom asked with a kind, yet penetrating, gaze.

"Yes. As a matter of fact, this morning, I was directed to the passage about how Abraham went out not knowing wither he went. I believe that is what I am to do as well…"

"Following the Lord one step at a time," Wisdom said, finishing the thought.

"Yes."

"I see. That is wise, and it is a plan that requires much faith, for there are many times men think they know which way is right, but the end of it is the way of death. I am glad to see that you do not want to follow your own thoughts in this."

"Definitely not," he replied with a small shake of his head.

"Let me ask you a question. Do you think this man you are seeking knows that he is called to bear the sword?"

Prayerful was a little taken aback at the question, for he had not even considered it. "I don't know.… Maybe the King has already spoken to him … maybe not."

"That is right. We do not know. That is what will make the search that much more difficult. So then, who is the only One that truly knows whom you should find?"

Without any hesitation, Prayerful answered, "The King certainly knows."

"Exactly. Thus, in order to find the man, you must first know and understand the heart of the Lord our King," she said, looking directly into his eyes.

There were a few moments of silence as Prayerful diverted his gaze and stared blankly at the lush grass while contemplating what she had just said. He was certainly not expecting such advice and was a little dumbfounded by it. He knew that as a Pilgrim he had his citizenship in the Celestial City and that he could pray to the Lord and read His Word, but how could one really get to know the King without seeing

Him face to face?   Prayerful decided to pose this question as he continued to stare at the ground, "How is it possible to *truly* know Him when He dwells in the Celestial City — not here? Isn't it impossible to know the Lord *that* well?"

"What do we read? Didn't God speak to Moses as a man speaks to his friend? Didn't Enoch walk with God? How about Samuel? God spoke with him in his ear. Elijah also heard the Lord's still small voice. There are many other examples I could give you, but I think you get the point: it certainly *is* possible to know God that deeply."

Prayerful was stunned by such a thought and began to wonder, *Can I ... can I truly know Him that closely?* Prayerful snapped his gaze back up and looked her in the eyes as his next question flowed without hesitation, "How can I get to know him more?"

"You must go down the Road of Seeking. One of the first men who took this road was Enoch, but others have traveled that way as well. Sadly, the further you go, the less it is trodden, for many have either given up or lost their focus.

"As you travel, you will get deeper and deeper into the mountains. The trail ends at the summit of Near-to-God Mountain where only a few have walked. The closer you get to the end of your journey, the better you will know your King, and also, you will discover where to find your man. Do not forget, the most wonderful thing in life is that we may know Him."

The thought of having such a relationship with the King sent shivers up Prayerful's spine, especially when he dwelled on the fact that his mission would take him to Near-to-God Mountain. *Wow! I can't believe I have been called to this! I wonder how many know that there is a way to that mountain.... How many know it even exists?*

Wisdom interrupted his thoughts when she said, "Your former journey was wonderful, but this one will have greater rewards and blessings. Let me warn you, though," she continued, "the way will be even more dangerous and difficult than your first trip with Believer."

"How so?"

"For one thing, the enemy's traps are created with even greater subtlety. It is difficult for many to notice some of these dangers since they are so alluring and seemingly innocent. Also, when our adversary does attack, he will do so with greater ferocity than you have already experienced. He does not want you to reach the top of the mountain and will do whatever he can to stop you. As a matter of fact, the further you go, the more you can expect trials and dangers that might hinder your progress. You must be always watching and praying; God will take care of you and give you the grace you need."

Prayerful, though a little intimidated by the greatness of the call and the enormity of the challenge, did not cower from going down the Road of Seeking, but instead his heart throbbed with determination to not fail His Lord. Prayerful lifted his head and gazed at the sky, resolving to do his utmost to accomplish the goal.

Prayerful looked back at Wisdom and asked, "Where is the beginning of the Road of Seeking?"

Madam Wisdom explained that he must first return to the Stream of Humility, and then head northeast through the Fields of Hungering. She then described specific landmarks for him to locate in order to find the road.

"This journey must not be delayed. The more one waits, the less likely he is to take the trip at all.... You should begin immediately," she said, pointing toward the northeast.

Heeding her advice, Prayerful stood up to go, saying, "Thank you for your help. I will head out immediately."

Wisdom, as well, arose with another question, "One more thing: are you prepared for the Forest of Daily Life?"

Prayerful had heard of that place before, but knew very little about it. "I guess so," he shrugged. "I did bring supplies for my journey," he said pointing to his bag.

"I don't think you know what I am talking about," she replied. "The Forest of Daily Life has very fertile soil, thus the trees of Required Responsibilities grow very quickly there.   The problem is that the ground there is so soft that the trees often topple over, littering the entire area in a tangled mass of branches and logs."

"Do you think the way will be blocked?" he asked, understanding the problem.

"It certainly is possible. The King has sent many workers there to keep the road open; however, the Storms of Difficulties and the Unexpected Winds often pound the area, wreaking havoc and making it difficult for anyone to keep going. You should have an axe in case there are fallen trees across the path."

"Alright," Prayerful said. "Where can I get one?"

"I will give you one," Wisdom offered.

"I don't want to take yours," Prayerful replied, not wanting to take advantage of her generosity.

"It is alright; I have a supply of them from the King Himself. They are for anyone who sets his face toward Near-to-God Mountain."

"Thank you.… I guess I will definitely need it," he admitted.

Wisdom led Prayerful around to the front of the house as she sent a servant to get the tool. In a few minutes, the man returned with a short-handled axe and a sharpening stone.

"Your sword will never lose its edge, because it is made of the everlasting Steel of Truth and designed by the King himself," Wisdom explained. "This axe, however, will get dull. The Lord has required that whenever I give someone an axe, I also give a sharpening stone."

Prayerful put the stone into his bag, then took the axe in hand and examined it. On the handle he saw a word carved into the wood: Work. Although he did not know how critical this tool would be, he strapped its sheath to his belt on the opposite side of his sword and was ready to go.

He thanked Wisdom for her helpful advice and tools, knowing that the things he gleaned from her today were invaluable. Turning around to leave, Prayerful took a deep breath and steeled himself for the greatest challenge he had ever faced.

As he walked toward the gate, he noticed that there was something written in stone next to the wall. It was placed in such a way that it would only be seen as one leaves Wisdom's house. The sign read:

Thus saith the LORD, Let not the wise man glory in his wisdom…. But let him that glorieth glory in this, that he understandeth and knoweth me.

Company

Although the day was almost half-spent, Prayerful began his long trek without delay. It did not take him much time to get to the stream, and then from there he turned northeast and journeyed through the green meadowland. Passing by several fields, he occasionally stopped for a drink from his canteen while watching the farmers plant their fields.

After an hour on the road, he finally spotted the first landmark that Wisdom told him about. In front of him and a little to the right, Eternal View Hill popped out of the plain like a lone stack of hay in a freshly mowed field. Although Wisdom had given a thorough description of it, Prayerful did not expect it to be as tall as it was. Wisdom explained that this was an important location, for only here could he get a glimpse of his goal. This would help him plan and prepare for the journey as best as he could; however, all of the planning in the world could not prepare him for the difficulties he would face.

After crossing through several fields, he came to the base of the hill and was soon ascending its slope. He was very thankful that he had not packed anything more than he did, for extra weight would certainly have slowed him down. Still, however, he knew that he would need a break once he reached the top.

Throughout the entire ascent, he enjoyed looking around at the beauty of the countryside. The grassy slope was dotted with a few trees that sprang up among a blanket of beautiful, purple flowers. As he looked around, he noticed that the further he went up the hill, the fewer the trees, but the landscape was still quite picturesque. He wanted to be able to stay here for a while to soak in the beauty around him, but he needed to press on.

Once he reached the top of the hill, Prayerful gasped in wonder at the view before him, for across the grassy hilltop, he could see many, many miles into the distance. On the other side of Eternal View Hill, further down the road, the green plains gradually gave way to woodland, and then even further in the distance, Prayerful noticed that the terrain grew more hilly, and, eventually, mountainous. Far off in the distance, an enormous mountain stood far above any other peak around it. *That must be Near-to-God Mountain*, he thought. *It looks like it will be quite a journey to get there.*

Prayerful found a rock nearby to sit on for a quick break. When he approached it, he noticed that the boulder was named Consider Your Ways. As he rested his weary legs, he pondered his future.

His thoughts soon drifted toward his own insignificance and inability. He did not have much training with the sword nor battle experience as others did. This, along with the fact that he was a short man with a very lean build, brought a wave of humility and thanksgiving to his heart — he certainly was not a great warrior … but at least he could be a messenger. He was joyful for the opportunity to serve his King and do something truly worthwhile; yet, he wondered, *Why would the Lord want someone as small as me to do such a monumental task?* He bowed his head in prayer for a few minutes, knowing that the job ahead was too great for him alone.

Soon, he stood back up, ready to press on and cover as much distance as possible before dark. Within a few minutes, he had crossed over to the other end of the hill and began descending the Slope of Desire. The excitement of the journey once again welled up within him so much that he soon began running down the hill. He wanted to shout for joy and began to wish that he could finish the rest of his trek at this speed.

Reaching the base of the hill, he slowed back down to a walk, gradually catching his breath again. Within a few yards of hiking on level ground, Prayerful saw a road ahead of him with a sign next to it: The Road of Seeking. Off to the left, another thoroughfare led away from this path; its sign declared the name: I Don't Care. For him, there was no choice as to which way he would take.

The Road of Seeking certainly was pleasant and offered him quite a bit of time to enjoy the peaceful silence of nature; the only sounds he heard were the singing of the birds and the occasional rustling of leaves in the wind. He continued on the path for a time and soon entered a young hardwood forest. The shade of the trees and the moist, outdoor air added to the serenity of this place.

Suddenly, the peaceful quiet was interrupted by a surprisingly loud growl. Prayerful's stomach shouted an audible protest, for, evidently, in his excitement on the top of the hill, he forgot to eat his mid-day meal and by now he was famished. While his stomach was crying out for food, his dry tongue begged him to take a long drink from his canteen.

Knowing that he had only one loaf of bread, Prayerful debated whether he should stop now to eat it, or save it till he set up camp for the night. If he ate it now, it would be difficult for him to find food in the evening when it would be getting dark, yet he hated to go any further on an empty stomach.

As he contemplated the best course of action, the answer to his dilemma lay around the next bend in the road, leaving Prayerful pleasantly surprised. There, a gentle stream babbled along next to the path for few hundred yards before twisting its way back into the woods. Near the gentle stream, a large tree stood, overladen with ripe fruit. Prayerful immediately recognized this as one of the trees planted by the King for those who hunger and thirst after righteousness. Though the fruit itself was not very big, it was known to be very sweet and satisfying.

He walked up to one of the lower branches, picked some fruit, and began to eat. The sweetness of the first bite was a little shocking to his tongue, but at the same time, it made his mouth water for more. He gladly finished the piece of fruit in his hand, and then picked and ate several more. After a few minutes of enjoying the luscious fruit, he went over to the stream and drank some of the cool, refreshing water. Still feeling a little hungry, he returned to the tree and helped himself to the fruit until he was completely satisfied.

Since he did not know how often he would be able to locate food on his trip, he decided to collect as much fruit as possible and keep it in his bag. The cooking pot was the first place that he thought of to store the food, and after that was full, he packed the fruit into any other area of his bag that he could find space. Even if he could not finish the fruit right away, it could be sliced, dried, and saved for later. Soon, his bag could hold no more.

As he was heading over to the stream to refill his canteen and get one more drink, he faintly heard some chatter from people coming down the trail toward him from the direction of Eternal View Hill. He bent over and took several swallows from the stream and then filled his canteen. When he stood up after replenishing his water supply, he gazed back down the trail to see who was coming. The voices were growing louder and more distinct, and within a minute, three people came around the bend in the road.

Prayerful almost dropped his canteen in surprise when he saw that the travelers were none other than Steadfast, Gentleness, and another one of Prayerful's neighbors, Half-Heart. All three looked as if they were prepared for a long trip and were fully armed. Prayerful waived at them, and they returned the gesture with a look of delight.

When they got a little closer, Prayerful asked, "What are you guys doing way out here?"

Steadfast replied for the group, "We have come to join you." Prayerful was taken aback at this announcement and could not hide the surprise on his face. Steadfast explained, "After you left this morning, Gentleness and I began to talk about your decision. We both agreed that our hearts were longing for more as well, and we could not stand by waiting out the rest of our time here doing nothing. Our prayer was 'Thy face, Lord, will I seek.'" Prayerful was stunned and he knew that his friends would not make such a decision lightly.

"Well," Steadfast continued, "we both got ready as quickly as we could and packed what things we could think of." Steadfast patted the pack on his right hip then finished, "When we were heading out, Half-Heart saw us and asked where we were going."

Interrupting, Half-Heart excitedly continued the story, "They told me all about your visitor. The whole thing sounded thrilling to me, and I knew in an instant that I wanted to go as well. I asked them to wait for me while I went into my house and got my things. I was ready to go in fifteen minutes, and we set out immediately." Without pausing for breath, he continued, "I agree with you that life is too short to spend just sitting around. I came through the wicket gate and to the cross about a year ago, and I have had my share of struggles and trials; but I thought that going on such a trip as this would really help me grow as a Pilgrim. Not only do I want to be more like Christ and know Him deeply, but I also thought that I could help you in your mission."

"We really want to go with you!" Gentleness added after a slight pause. "We will help you in any way possible."

How could he refuse such an offer? "Well, Scripture says that two are better than one," Prayerful stated. "I guess if there are four of us, then that is definitely better than one." He smiled and opened his arms wide in invitation, "I would love to have you join me!"

The three new companions seemed quite excited to be taking such a journey, and Prayerful, himself, was relieved that he did not have to go on alone. Prayerful, however, had one more question, "How did you know where to find me? When I left, I told you I didn't know where I was supposed to go."

Steadfast answered, "That was easy; we went to Wisdom, and she gave us the same directions that she gave you. We figured that if we kept gong at a quick pace, we would eventually catch up to you, and … well … here we are," he said with a smile.

"I see," Prayerful stated as his eyes filled with understanding.

"Speaking of moving, shouldn't we be on our way?" Half-Heart stated as he glanced down the trail. "I think we would want to get as far as we could before dusk.... After all, the King's business should not be delayed."

"True," Prayerful replied. "However, I think we should first stock up on food while we can." Pointing with his thumb to the nearby tree, he continued, "I have already loaded my bag with as much fruit as I can carry; I suggest you all do the same. There is no guarantee that we will always be able to get food so easily."

The other three agreed and soon bags were being filled with the prized fruit. After only a few minutes, Half-Heart took a pause from picking and asked to hold Passionate's sword. Prayerful agreed, unsheathed it, and handed it to him. As he held it, Half-Heart seemed mesmerized by the glimmering weapon, examining every detail. He even made a few comments to himself how this weapon had been in many battles and had been carried by the most faithful of men.

Prayerful noticed that Steadfast paused in his fruit-gathering, glanced at Half-Heart, and shook his head at this man's fixation with the sword. At this subtle gesture, Prayerful began to wonder how Steadfast's serious and thoughtful nature would mesh with Half-Heart's typical lack of dedication, despite times of great enthusiasm. He hoped that there would not be friction between the two of them.

Soon, Half-Heart returned the sword and resumed gathering fruit. Throughout their time working around the tree, Prayerful could not help but notice that Half-Heart's bag was a bit bigger and more heavily loaded than the others. Their friend, evidently, did not understand the need to travel light, and Prayerful wondered if this would eventually become a problem. He grew even more concerned when he happened to see some of the things in the bag — several of the items were completely unnecessary. The one that caused the most concern was a magazine called *Serving Two Masters*. Prayerful was tempted to say something but did not think it best at the moment.

When their bags were completely full, the four of them were ready to press on. As they walked together, Prayerful began to notice that Half-Heart did, indeed, have trouble keeping up with them, but, thankfully, he did not slow them down too much.

As the trail wound its way through the young hardwood forest, the four friends enjoyed the peaceful afternoon and chatted as they went. They talked of various things, from their previous journeys to their life by the river.

Later in the afternoon, after a slight break in their conversation, Steadfast said to Prayerful, "By the way, Wisdom also gave me an axe and said that you would explain the reason for it."

"Oh, I didn't even notice you had it!" Prayerful said as he glanced at the tool hanging at Steadfast's side. "It will definitely be good to have two of them. She warned me that we will need them in the Forest of Daily Life." Prayerful went on to repeat Wisdom's explanation of that woodland and everyone was thankful for the advanced warning.

As the sun slid down toward the horizon and crept behind the western hills, Prayerful declared that they should make camp before it got too dark. Looking around, they soon found a place near the road that seemed ideal for the four of them. The men worked together to gather wood and start a fire, while

Gentleness set to work preparing a simple supper of bread, fruit, and some dried meat that she had packed in her bag.

As darkness took over the countryside, the four friends sat around the crackling fire, enjoying their simple meal and resting their weary feet. After they were done eating, Prayerful took some time to describe what he was told about the journey to Near-to-God Mountain. He then went on to explain that, since they did not know who would eventually carry Passionate's sword, Near-to-God Mountain may not be their final destination. For all he knew, the man whom they were seeking could be in any town or village, and they needed to be prepared to travel on a second journey, possibly even to the far reaches of the land. The three of them nodded their heads in understanding.

As the peaceful night sounds began to be heard throughout the woods and the half moon dimly lit the forest floor, Half-Heart declared that he was going to hit the sack. Gentleness, too, decided it was time to go to sleep, and she went off to her bedroll. Steadfast and Prayerful were both grateful that the others went to bed, for they wanted some time to talk to each other alone.

"I almost didn't let Half-Heart come," Steadfast whispered once he heard Half-Heart snoring. "I am afraid he will either slow us down or get sidetracked, and then we will have to go after him." Prayerful could hear the edge of concern in his voice.

"I know," Prayerful answered. "I have already noticed that he has brought too much with him. He seems to be more interested in laying up treasure upon earth than in heaven."

"Yes. I just didn't know how to say, 'No,' … especially since he was so eager."

"Well, I understand…. He certainly can be quite

insistent when he sets his mind on something."

Steadfast chuckled, "That certainly is true."

"Well, let's hope for the best. Maybe this trip will help him mature."

"I hope so. About the only thing that can truly change such a person is a meeting with the King."

"Yes.... Well, I guess, in the mean time, we will need to do our best to be patient with him. After all, growth does take time."

"And a willingness to let God have his way," Steadfast added.

"True," Prayerful replied, understanding Steadfast's reservation. After a few moments, he added, "Well, I think we need to be extra careful that we do not let his typical lack of dedication impact the rest of us. A little leaven will leaven the whole lump."

"I agree," Steadfast replied, his mind obviously thinking on something else. After a minute of silence, Steadfast voiced his thoughts, "You know, you always spoke of how you and Believer would often practice with your swords to help keep your focus and skill up. Maybe we should do the same — all of us. It is probably the best way to combat any apathy."

"True. It would definitely be good.... It certainly helped in my journey with Believer.... I think we can start tomorrow morning."

Steadfast yawned, "Good. Well, I need to get some sleep."

"Me too," Prayerful agreed as they both stood up.

They added some more wood to the fire, and then both went to their place to lay down for the night. As he rested his head on the softest part of his pack, Prayerful had a contented smile on his face despite the concerns over their one companion. As he glanced at the glowing fire, he once again played the messenger's words in his mind.   Before long, his heavy eyes and weary body drew him to sleep.

Trapped

The four friends trudged along the dirt road in silence, listening to the melody of the chirping birds in the distance.   Prayerful was glad for the quiet this morning because he needed some time to think; he had not been able to have much solitude since his friends joined him yesterday.   If they were going to make this whole trip together through all sorts of danger and trials, he needed to know how they could all work as a team, for they each had their own unique strengths and weaknesses.

When the three others had initially joined him on this mission, Prayerful was concerned that there would be a good bit of friction between Steadfast and Half-Heart.   He was quite relieved, however, to find that Steadfast was working very hard to be patient.   This man certainly had a good head on his shoulders and a heart that always sought to do the right thing with the right attitude; Steadfast was a very consistent and stable man.   Prayerful also knew that this man's larger build and strong frame would be very helpful if they ran into trouble, not to mention that his skill with the sword could be invaluable when facing enemies.   Prayerful figured that he would be relying heavily on this friend in the days to come.

As far as Gentleness was concerned, her gifts were with medicine. She had always been one to help those who were sick, and Prayerful knew that if they had any injuries or illness, she would know what to do. Her greatest contribution, however, was that she had a sweet spirit and a tender, trusting heart. Not only did she speak compassionately to everyone around her, but she always thought of others first, doing what she could to help and serve them.

Prayerful remained cautiously optimistic about Half-Heart's role in their team, but thus far, this fourth member of the group had done his best to help out. Prayerful was thankful that he did seem to have some measure of zeal and spoke often of the King, encouraging everyone to press on. *But will this continue?* Prayerful wondered. He knew that Half-Heart could easily be distracted, and may even go off on some other "adventure." He tended to be zealous about things for a little while but rarely followed them through to completion. At least for the moment, he seemed to be doing well; Prayerful just had to keep him focused.

Prayerful's mind then shifted away from the members of the team to another topic: their supplies. Everyone had packed his own cloak and a supply of food, water, and eating utensils. Steadfast had also brought along a short rope and a fishing line along with his own tinderbox.

Gentleness had a few medical supplies in her pack and was prepared for most emergencies. She also brought along a small skillet, and had filled her bag with as many spices and dried goods as possible. At least their meals would not be bland.

Although Prayerful did not know everything that Half-Heart had loaded in his bag, he was aware that he had his bedroll and a small knife. Half-Heart, evidently, was in such a rush when he packed that he did not think through what would be needed for the journey, and as a result, he did not have much to contribute.

Thinking on their list of supplies brought a smile of satisfaction to Prayerful knowing that their daily needs would be met as well as preparation for emergencies. Food could be gathered or purchased along the way, and they could easily make some sort of shelter to protect them from rain when they were far from civilization. Even though they would not have all of the comforts of life, they did not lack any necessity.

"I am guessing that those trees over there mark the beginning of the Forest of Daily Life," Half-Heart said, interrupting Prayerful's thoughts. Everyone gazed up the trail to where he was pointing and saw a mixture of enormous hardwoods and softwoods forming a boundary against the fields they had been traveling through. They all stared in awe at the massive forest that loomed before them.

"I believe you are right," Steadfast replied. "I have heard that it is so vast that if one tries to explore off the trail, he could easily get lost and never find his way out."

"Well, we must be careful, then, to stay on the road," Gentleness commented.

Half-Heart added with a look of determination, "I guess we are about to find out if everything we have heard about this place is true. We will have to just keep plugging along no matter what we face."

Within a few minutes, the four friends approached the edge of the forest; then, without looking back, they entered into the dimness of the great wood. The thick foliage above their heads made it difficult to discern the location of the sun, but at the same time, the shade felt good.

They had not gone far before everyone noticed that on either side of the trail an unnumbered amount of trees lay on the ground, creating a ten-foot-high layer of thick brush, branches, and logs as far as the eye could see down the road. They eventually learned that this tangle of fallen trees continued on for the full length of these woods. However, the mess of trees did make it very easy to see the cleared roadway.

As they were plodding along, gazing at the massive trees, all of a sudden, a great rumble began in the distance, and then a *crash* echoed through the forest. Within moments, they realized that somewhere in the woods, another great tree was now added to the tangled mess on the forest floor. This would become a noise which they would hear far too often on this part of their journey.

After they traveled further into the forest, Half-Hart asked, "These trees are a little different from what I am used to. Does anyone recognize them?"

"Yes," Steadfast replied. Pointing to the right, he said, "Over there, you can see the Hemlock of Household Chores; right next to it is a Birch of Meal Preparation."

"What is that big one over there?" Prayerful questioned while pointing to an enormous hardwood on their left.

"That is a Maple of Employment, and the one next to it is a Hobby Hickory. As you can tell, there are many different types and sizes of trees in this forest. I certainly can't name them all.... In fact, I believe that there are very few woodsmen who could name even a majority of them."

"I wonder why these trees fall so easily," Half-

Heart stated.

"I have been told that all the trees in this forest are unique in that they have small root systems that will not penetrate very deep into the soil." Steadfast stated. When any kind of wind or rain comes along, it is very easy for them to fall since they do not have much of a foundation."

"Why are there so many trees still standing if they can fall so easily? Wouldn't all the trees have been blown over by now?" Gentleness asked.

"Well, you see, the soil is so rich that new trees are able to grow very quickly," Steadfast answered. "The trees that you are looking at are much younger than you might think; some of them may only be a few years old. New trees quickly fill in the places of those that have fallen."

"I guess it makes sense why there is such a problem with the trail getting blocked," Prayerful commented.

The group walked throughout the rest of the day and occasionally heard more trees come crashing down in the distance. As they observed darkness slowly creep into the woods, they were on the constant lookout for a safe place to sleep that night; the thought of sleeping on the open trail made everyone nervous. Without seeing many options, they soon decided that the best thing that they could do would be to make a shelter under one of the larger fallen trees that littered the side of the road.

As they continued on, searching for the right spot to make camp, Half-Heart shouted, "Look over there! Do you see what I see?"

The others all gazed in the direction that he was pointing. Next to the trail a few yards ahead, the bare face of rock stood out of the hillside. Right in the middle of it was an opening to a cave called Rest; they had found a safe place after all. Everyone quickly hiked over to the six-foot-wide opening in the rock ledge and entered the dim cavern. They found it to be a very suitable place to sleep with ample room to move about. In the darkness of the cave, they each claimed a portion of the dirt floor and set their belongings down.

Wanting to know more about this place, Prayerful took out his lamp and lit it. As the warm light filled the underground chamber, the entire group realized that this was not a natural cave but a man-made cavern. Chiseled into the back wall, they all read the words, "Come unto me, all ye that labour and are heavy laden, and I will give you rest."

Looking around, they could see that the space was clearly designed for people to sleep comfortably. There was even a small, underground stream in the back of the cave; there would be no lack of fresh water here. They quickly took note that there was even a fire pit already built with dry wood off to the side. Though everyone was quite weary from the long day, they all smiled, knowing that the Lord always supplied their needs, even in a place such as this. They ate a simple supper, and soon everyone lay down for the night. Before long, they had all fallen asleep oblivious to the fact that a storm was brewing outside.

*   *   *

A mighty, thunderous crash jolted everyone awake; Half-Heart and Prayerful shot upright and everyone's heart raced wildly. Although they could not see because of the darkness of the night, they could hear the overwhelming sound of strong winds rushing through the forest as the sky poured out a torrent of rain. Instantly, they realized that the noise that jolted them out of sleep was not thunder but a tree somewhere close to their cave that had come crashing down.

Half-Heart voiced his concern, "That tree might be across our path.... It might even be blocking the entrance to the cave.... It sure sounded close enough.... We might be trapped here!"

"That is true," Prayerful added, as his own memory affirmed the nearness of the crash.

"Do you think we should go investigate? After all, if it is blocking us in, we could be stuck here for days," Half-Heart lamented.

"I don't think we need to, Half-Heart," Steadfast replied as they heard another tree join its fallen comrades on the forest floor. "It will be there in the morning, and there is nothing we can do about it now anyway.... I think we should just try to get some more rest. Worrying about it won't help anything," he added with a yawn, "but it will make us quite exhausted tomorrow."

The others agreed with this suggestion, and everyone hoped that their fears would be for nought. As Prayerful laid his head back down on his sack, listening to several other trees fall in the woods, he wondered how he could get back to sleep — his heart was still racing, and his mind wanted to dwell on what they might find in the morning. *Who knows how many trees may have fallen across the path,* he thought. It was difficult, but Prayerful tried not to dwell on such worries. Although it took a while, he eventually relaxed and drifted off to sleep till morning.

*   *   *

As the sun illumined the woodland the following morning, Gentleness lit a fire to start breakfast while the men went out to survey the damage. Their hearts fell when they beheld the scene outside of the cave; the pathway was completely blocked by a thick tangle of branches from several fallen hardwood. It turned out that when the one tree came down, it took a number of others with it. They were definitely stuck here for a while; there was no way they could even climb over such a mess.

Trying to hide his own discouragement, Prayerful remarked, "Well, I guess it is a good thing that Wisdom gave us the axes."

"It will take forever to clear all of this," moaned Half-Heart as he motioned with his hand toward the tangled trees.

"Well, with all of us working together, we will have it done before you know it," replied Steadfast with a slight smile, trying to remain optimistic.

The three turned around and entered the cave again, determined that they would clear up the mess quickly. Half-Heart walked over to Steadfast's axe and picked it up saying, "I don't like the idea of being trapped." Turning to Steadfast he declared, "I will work for a while."

"What about breakfast?" questioned Gentleness as she looked up from the meal she was preparing.

"I am fine. There is too much to do right now." With that, he marched out of the cave, and within moments, he began working at a large maple limb. Not wanting his friend to work alone, Prayerful picked up his axe and soon was working on the tree as well. After they ate, Steadfast and Gentleness joined them to help drag the cut branches away and throw them off the path. Progress was slow and tiring.

Prayerful and Half-Heart continued working for several hours, refusing to take a break. By the time noon came, they had not made much progress and were quite discouraged. Steadfast insisted that they go in for a break and food; this time, Half-Heart agreed.

After an hour of rest, Half-Heart got back up and exited the cave to resume the work. With every whack of Half-Heart's axe, Prayerful grew in despair as he sat on the dirt floor next to the crackling fire. He stared at the axe he had been using and wondered how long they would be trapped. The word "Work" on the handle seemed to stare back at him and mock their slow progress. *Why is it taking so long to get these trees cleaned up? Certainly with two of us, we should be moving more quickly.*

Steadfast came up to Prayerful, picked up the axe, and looked down on his friend. "Don't worry, we will get it cleared," he affirmed. "I will chop for a while and give you a break."   Prayerful was somewhat relieved by this, for his arms already felt like jelly. As Steadfast was about to leave the cave, he stopped and examined the axe for a few moments.

"This thing is extremely dull!" he stated.

"Really?"

"Yes.   No wonder you weren't getting much done."

"What do you mean?"

"The sharper the axe, the deeper it will penetrate into the wood with each swing. A dull axe can be almost worthless, and it will make the work much harder and take you that much longer. I better put a good edge on this before I head out."

"Let me get you the sharpening stone," Prayerful offered, encouraged by the thought that their progress could speed up.

He retrieved the stone from his bag and noticed that several words were etched in its side: "Time With

God." He then handed it to Steadfast who kneeled down and began to methodically work a sharp edge back onto the axe.

Before long, Half-Heart came storming back into the cave and yelled, "Am I going to work alone?! Why are you guys just sitting around?!"

Steadfast looked up at him and said, "The axe is dull and desperately needs to be sharpened."

"It doesn't make that much of a difference," Half-Heart retorted. "As long as you keep swinging in the right place, the weight of the axe head will do the job."

"You are wasting a lot of time if you don't get that thing sharpened," Steadfast replied as he nodded to the axe in Half-Heart's hand.

Half-Heart huffed and stormed back out, unwilling to listen. When he began chopping again, it seemed to Prayerful that he was hitting the tree with more aggression than before. Prayerful did feel a little guilty for allowing Half-Heart to work alone, so he got up and went back out to help. Gentleness followed as well, and soon they were continuing their task of clearing what had been cut.

Before long, Steadfast emerged from the cave, carrying the newly sharpened axe, and approached the tree. He selected a large limb, lifted the axe high into the air, and began working away at the wood. Within a few minutes, Prayerful looked over at Steadfast and was shocked when he saw that he had severed one medium-sized limb and had already begun working on another.

Over the next hour, Prayerful grew amazed at how quickly Steadfast was getting things done. After a couple more hours (and several more times that Steadfast took a break to sharpen the axe), they were finished with the first tree and had moved on to the next one. It was certainly clear that Steadfast was getting more accomplished, but Half-Heart excused it away by saying that Steadfast was much stronger. Through it all, Half-Heart refused to admit that the sharpened edge had anything to do with their success; rather, he often complained that Steadfast was wasting time by sharpening it so often.

Everyone continued to work though the rest of the day and were worn out by the time the sun was setting. Being so fatigued, they knew that they would sleep well that night and decided to get to bed as soon as possible. Though they did not get as much done as they were hoping, they had made a good bit of progress.

When Prayerful awoke the next morning, he decided to not relive the mistakes they had made the previous day. Not only had they wasted a good bit of time with dull axes, but they had also neglected their sword practice. Prayerful spent some time reading his Bible, and then picked up his sword and went outside for their daily drills.

Half-Heart was impatient and decided only to watch as Steadfast, Gentleness, and Prayerful took their time with the practice session. Then, after breakfast, Prayerful and Steadfast took even more time to sharpen both of the axes, much to Half-Heart's annoyed impatience. Although Prayerful could feel the tension in the cave, he knew that he needed to do what was right.

Once again, the sound of chopping echoed through the woods as the men set to work. Within several hours, they had cleared the second tree out of the way. After lunch, they finished the last small oak, and their way was open.

Though the day was half spent, there was no question as to whether they should proceed with their journey or not. Their things were packed quickly, and in a short amount of time, the four friends were on the road again. They hoped that they would not have to clear too many trees in the near future, but if the need arose, at least they would be ready for it.

Voices in the Woods

"How much longer do you think we will be in these woods?" Half-Heart questioned as they trudged along the trail.

"I'm not exactly sure," Prayerful answered, "But I think we will be out of here before long … hopefully within two days."

It had been just over a week since they had first had to deal with the fallen trees of the Forest of Daily Life, and by now, they had cleared more trees than they wished to remember. Most of the time, the tops of the trees or a few large branches was all that they had to deal with, but there were times they had to take care of the entire trunk as well.

The four companions had been able to find a cave every night, and, thankfully, there were no more storms despite the constant threat in the skies above. Only once did a strong wind blow through, wreaking havoc in the forest, but it had not been too severe of a job to clean up. Typically, they did not have to spend more than half a day at most clearing the mess and were thankfully able to keep moving.

On this particular day, as they were plodding along, enjoying each other's conversation, Gentleness suddenly stopped in her tracks for a moment, and then asked, "Do you hear something?"

Everyone else paused as well and listened for a few moments. "I don't hear anything," Half-Heart eventually declared.

"Maybe it was just my imagination," she stated.

They resumed their former pace down the wooded trail, picking up their former conversation of the perils of the City of Vanity. Before long, Gentleness stopped, furrowed her eyebrows, and stated, "I heard it again.... I am certain this time."

They all stopped once more and listened. Prayerful could hear some leaves rustle in the wind, along with the chirping of songbirds in the distance, but he could not pick out anything unusual. "What did it sound like?" he asked.

"It sounded almost like someone chopping wood," she explained.

Again, they strained their ears to listen and for a few moments, they only heard the silence of the forest, but soon, Prayerful began to distinguish a faint, methodic *chop, chop, chop.* "I think I can hear it, too," he declared. "It sounds like it is somewhere down the trail in front of us."

"There probably is a tree across the path ahead, and another Pilgrim is trying to get through," Steadfast theorized.

"Well, let's go and see if they need help," Half-Heart stated abruptly as he took off, marching down the trail. Everyone else joined him and silently proceeded, listening for more indicators of where the person may be.

After a few minutes, they stopped again to listen; however, this time, everything was silent. They all looked at one another in confusion, not knowing what to do next and even wondering if their imagination had been playing tricks on them. All of a sudden, a voice echoed in the distance, and a second person replied. Then, a third man began laughing.

"Whoever they are, maybe they would like to join us," Half-Heart said hopefully.

"As long as they are Pilgrims heading to Near-to-God Mountain, we might end up with quite a group by the time we are done," Prayerful answered, hoping for more company.

As they continued on, heading further down the road, the voices grew louder and more distinct. Strangely enough, the four of them also began to notice that these people seemed to be off the road to their right. *Maybe the path will take a sharp turn*, thought Prayerful; however, the road continued to lead them on a relatively straight course. Soon, it became very evident that the men who were working in the woods were not on the trail at all but were in the woods itself, lost in a dense jungle of fallen trees.

Prayerful halted, and the four of them looked at the high wall of tangled branches on the right side of the road while they listened to the voices in the distance. The strangers were too far off the trail for Prayerful to make out their conversation but close enough to distinguish specific words here and there.

Steadfast cupped his hands around his mouth and shouted, "Hello!"

There was not an immediate response, but before Steadfast attempted a second greeting, they saw three powerfully built men climbing trees a couple dozen yards off the main road. When these men spotted Prayerful's group, they shouted back, "Hello, there." Then, they each found a good branch in their tree to sit on and talk.

"Is everybody alright over there?" Prayerful asked.

The man who appeared to be the oldest gave a questioning look, and then answered, "Of course."

"Ok. We just didn't know if you needed help or not," Prayerful replied.

"Oh, no, we are fine. It will just take us quite a while to get out of here."

"How did you get into such a predicament?"

One of the younger men responded, "Well, we are Pilgrims, and about a year ago, we decided to make the trek to Near-to-God Mountain. So, we left our home town of Manpower and set out.... Everything seemed to be going well for a while."

The third man continued the story with his gravelly voice, "When we came to these woods, we were able to travel for several days. One night, a bad storm blew through, knocking down many trees. We started working right away, and we have been clearing the path ever since." He gave a slight pause, and then added, "By the way, I am Workaholic. That is Labor-First," he said, pointing to the man to his right. "And this is Love-of-Work," he declared as he pointed to the oldest man who was to his left.

Prayerful introduced the members of his group, and then said, "It sounds like you have been working for quite a long time."

"Yea, but we think that this is the best thing we can do in our service to God.... I am sure that He is pleased with us. One day, we will reach Near-to-God Mountain, but for now, we've got a lot to do."

"Aren't you afraid that you are going too slow and will never get out? Are your axes sharp?" Steadfast questioned.

"We used to try to keep them sharp, but we

figured it was taking too much time to keep that edge, so we do not bother with it any more. In fact, a while ago, a man, Mr. Live-for-Now, came along and confirmed that sharpening is a waste of time." Prayerful stole a quick glance at his companions and noticed that Half-Heart gave a sideways glare toward Steadfast at this comment.

Workaholic continued the story, "Live-for-Now said that fifteen minutes spent sharpening the axe was fifteen minutes that could have been used clearing trees. Add the three of us together, and there was forty-five minutes a day that was being wasted. Anyway, not only did he give us good advice, but he also somehow made his way through the brush and generously traded our old, smaller axes for three really big ones."

"But if you don't keep them sharp," Steadfast reasoned, "they won't cut into the wood very well. It will take you a very long time to get out of here."

"We are doing just fine," Love-of-Work answered. "We have been doing so well that, over the last two months, we have even opened a small clearing next to the trail we have been working on…. It is a great place to put all of the firewood and logs we have cut. Even now, we are making another clearing, so we can store more wood."

"What about your journey to Near-to-God Mountain?" Prayerful asked.

"Well, we still would like to get there someday, but we have found that this work is more important for the moment. After all, we have quite a pile of wood, and once we get out of here, we are planning on selling it," he explained. "We decided to put our focus on logging for now because we think we might make quite a successful business out of it once we get out of these woods. Our hope is that we will even be able to support the Lord's work with what money we make."

"So then, have you forgotten your goal?" Half-Heart questioned.

"Which goal?" Labor First questioned, "Near-to-God Mountain? No, we haven't forgotten it.… We just have a different priority right now."

"Don't forget," Prayerful argued, "knowing God is the greatest thing imaginable. It is the highest goal you can ever reach."

"We know that!" Love-of-Work replied, obviously frustrated. He took a breath, trying to relax, and then continued, "We *are* still hoping to get there someday. We just have a different focus for now. Once we get out of here and have a large enough pile of wood to sell, we will press on to the mountain."

"But you have another problem," Prayerful added. "You are off the trail; the road is over here. If you don't get back on the trail, you could be going in circles trying to make your own way. You could be trapped here for the rest of your life."

"I think *you* are the ones off the trail," replied Workaholic with an edge of anger in his voice. "We have been working on this pathway for about a year.… I think we know what we are talking about. Look, we don't need anybody coming along, telling us that we are doing everything wrong. We are serving the Lord our way, and I believe that He is very happy with what we are doing."

"We are just trying to help," Prayerful replied, trying to calm the tense situation.

"We don't need your help, thank you!" Workaholic rebutted with a shout. "You have wasted enough of our time, and we need to get back to work. Good day." Without another word, the three woodcutters moved from their places in the trees and began climbing back down to the ground.

Prayerful and his friends were stunned as they watched the three men descend out of sight. Within minutes, the methodic sound of the chopping of axes echoed through the woods once again. Prayerful stood, staring blankly at the tangled mass of fallen trees while Steadfast simply shook his head over the foolishness of these men. Since there was nothing more they could do, the four companions turned and resumed their trek down the road.

"One thing is for sure," Steadfast declared once they were out of earshot of the loggers. "They will never get out of this place. They love their work so much that they have lost the goal of getting to the mountain."

"What I think is worse," Prayerful added, "is that they have deceived themselves into thinking that they are actually still serving God…. In reality, they are just serving themselves."

"What blindness!" Gentleness exclaimed with a pained expression on her face.

"It seems to me that they love to wear the guise of spirituality when they are actually filled with the love the world," Half-Heart theorized.

Hearing such words come from Half-Heart somewhat shocked Prayerful, especially since he knew that some of the things in Half-Heart's bag were a display of *his* love for the world. To accuse others of hypocrisy seemed very hypocritical of Half-Heart. Prayerful could not understand why his friend could not see the beam in his own eye while trying to pull the speck out of another's eye. *I guess the same is true of all of us. We often do not notice how bad we are until God points it out*, Prayerful thought.

"Is there any hope for those men?" Gentleness

asked.

"There is only one hope," Prayerful answered, turning back to the conversation at hand. "They need to listen to the King's Messenger, the Voice of Admonition, to get back on the trail. Then, they must set their sights on the mountain and press onward. If they don't heed, they will remain lost in the Forest of Daily Life, continually working for no profit."

The Town of Academia

Prayerful finished reading his Bible scroll and set it aside as the morning sun rose above the horizon. At the same instant, Steadfast stood up and girded on his weapon for their daily time of sword drills. Prayerful did the same, and soon the two of them walked out into the beautiful meadow that bordered their camp, with Gentleness following closely behind. Prayerful gave a slight shiver as the morning air was still cool, but at least their practice session would quickly warm him up.

Prayerful was glad that they had developed this habit of sword training while they were in the Forest of Daily Life, for it both honed their skills and it helped keep them focused on what was important. It had taken great discipline to pull out their swords every morning, especially when there was much work to be done, but they soon found that the rewards were great. Even though they had left that forest two days ago, they did not stop working with each other every morning, and Prayerful was sure that his swordsmanship was improving.

The men faced off, and soon the sound of clanging metal filled the region. Prayerful found that their training times were the highlight of his day. Many times, they would simply go back over the basics, but it was not uncommon for Steadfast to show the others a new maneuver.   Prayerful found that the skills that Believer had originally worked into him were being continually refined and sharpened by Steadfast.

Steadfast proved to be a master swordsman and an excellent teacher.   Prayerful eventually discovered that his comrade had been highly trained ever since he was a child and had been in several battles.   *This man certainly knows how to handle a sword very well*, Prayerful often thought.   Not only was Steadfast a good swordsman at the peak of physical fitness, but he also was a man with a genuine heart for the Lord.

That morning, while Steadfast and Gentleness were taking their turns practicing, Prayerful glanced over to where they had made camp the night before. Half-Heart was sitting under a nearby oak, watching the others practice while his own sword lay next to his bedroll, untouched since the previous day. It was also easy to see that he was not fully paying attention to Steadfast's instruction, but rather, his mind was somewhere else, his eyes staring off into the distance.

Prayerful was very concerned for his companion, for ever since their time in the Forest of Daily life, Half-Heart had only sporadically participated in their drills. Prayerful had hoped that once they left the woods behind that things would be different; however, since getting out of there two days ago, nothing had really changed. Prayerful was amazed how Half-Heart could talk about God so often, yet he did not want to put forth much effort in his practice. Prayerful knew that he had to do something to help his friend, so he quickly developed a plan to get Half-Heart to join in their drills — at least for one day.

When Steadfast sheathed his sword and began

walking back to the camp with Gentleness, Prayerful stayed behind in the field and called out, "Half-Heart, why don't you come over, and we will practice a little more. I have a few more things that I want to work on."

Half-Heart had a small stick in his hand which he threw to the side in a mild show of annoyance. Without a word, he got up, grabbed his weapon from among his belongings, and walked out to the field. Prayerful did not want to make it a lengthy session, but he wanted it to be just long enough to get Half-Heart's mind into it. He was hoping to rekindle his friend's interest in sword practice.

Prayerful raised his sword and positioned his feet; Half-Heart did the same. When Prayerful glanced at his friend, he groaned inside with frustration. *He still doesn't have his feet right…. He refuses to listen whenever I show him.* He decided to say nothing and just let it be for now since there were many other things they needed to work on.

They ran through a few basic maneuvers and then moved on to a few moderate ones. Prayerful's heart sank as he saw how much Half-Heart was struggling. He tended to attack recklessly and aggressively, seeming to just swing his sword back and forth with little thought; he knew some of the basics, but not much else.

While working through one specific move, Half-Heart, no matter what he did, could not accomplish what he had been shown. Prayerful wondered in frustration, *Will he ever get this?* Prayerful took a deep breath to calm down and focused on working with his friend. He hoped that they would not have to face enemies any time soon, for everyone else would have to work hard to protect Half-Heart.

They continued practicing for a few more

minutes before Prayerful decided they should finish. Half-Heart ended his last attack and sheathed his sword with a huff. Prayerful was disheartened as he realized that his attempt to rekindle the interest of sword practice in his friend had failed.

At that moment, a man nearby spoke up, "You need to twist your wrist." All four friends jumped and spun around, looking in the direction that the voice had come from. Instantly, they saw two men a few dozen yards away on the road. Apparently, these men had been watching the four of them practice and were thus able to approach unnoticed.

Everyone was still a little surprised by the presence of their visitors when the one man clarified what he said to Half-Heart, "With your last move, you should have twisted your wrist. Here, let me come show you."

The two strangers strode into the meadow and drew their swords for a demonstration. They showed step by step how a swordsman should twist the wrist of his sword hand at a specific time during the maneuver. Then, they had Half-Heart run it through several times until they were satisfied that he had the movements down.

Prayerful had never heard of such a thing and was a little unsure about its effectiveness, so he watched their session with curious scrutiny. During the demonstration, Prayerful glanced toward the camp to observe Steadfast's reaction and found him mildly scowling; something was not right. Half-Heart, on the other hand, was fully absorbed into what the men were saying; evidently, he did not care about practicing what he already knew but only wanted to learn new things.

"So, how will this help in a fight?" Half-Heart asked the strangers.

"If you twist your wrist while your arm is in that particular position, the edge of your blade will hit your opponent," the one man explained. "The way you did it before would make it so that you wouldn't have any contact with the enemy at all…. The edge of your sword would completely miss him." Half-Heart nodded in understanding.

When they were done giving their explanation, the man who initially corrected Half-Heart spoke, "I am Fill the Mind and this is Without Heart. We are from the Town of Academia just a few miles off this road."

Prayerful introduced their group, and then asked if the men were Pilgrims as well.

"Why, of course," Without Heart stated with an edge of condescension. "Can't you tell by how we are dressed?"

"I thought you might be," Prayerful responded as he took a second glance at the cross on Without Heart's tunic. "But I just wanted to make sure."

"Where did you learn to handle a weapon?" Steadfast questioned as he approached the men in the meadow.

"In Academia," Fill the Mind replied. "They have a large college there to train Pilgrims in the way of God. I think all of you would do well to stop there for a little while. You appear to be moderate swordsmen, and I think you should get more training."

"Thank you, but no" Steadfast replied. "We already have a journey to take, and we need to keep on going."

"Ok," Fill the Mind stated. "Just remember, you are always welcome to stop by. We have a lot of teachers who can help you, and I believe it would do you some good."

"Thank you," Prayerful said.

"Academia is a great stronghold filled with many Pilgrims who faithfully study God's Word. We all love to examine it and work very hard to know the smallest detail," Without Heart bragged.

"So then, how has your study impacted your life?" Steadfast asked. Prayerful sensed that his friend was asking this probing question to test these men.

"Oh, it has definitely changed our lives," Fill the Mind replied. "We spend so much time in study and in teaching others that I never would have done otherwise."

"But how has God changed your *hearts*?" Steadfast pressed.

"Well," Fill the Mind stammered, "we believe what is most important is what we know. That is why we have such a focus on our education, and ... I suppose that could be the answer to your question.... We have greatly grown in our knowledge of spiritual things."

"It is wonderful to gain more knowledge ... but if that knowledge does not have an impact upon our daily living, it is practically worthless," Steadfast explained. "If any man be in Christ, he is a new creature."

Prayerful could clearly tell both of these men were growing uncomfortable with Steadfast's words as they gave each other a sideways glance. "Well," Without Heart hesitated for a moment, trying to figure out what to say, "I don't think it is wise for you try to say that we aren't good Pilgrims. After all, we could run circles around you in a sword fight."   Prayerful almost chuckled, for, knowing Steadfast's expertise, he figured that his friend could easily beat these two in a matchup.

At this, Without Heart looked around at everyone, declaring, "Well, I am glad we could stop for a few minutes and give you some pointers, but we *do* need to be going."

"Yes," Fill the Mind explained, showing a little relief that they had an excuse to leave. "I am sorry, but we need to be on our way. We are heading to the village of Tickling the Ear to teach a class there about the fine points of swordsmanship."

"I see," Prayerful replied.

"It was nice to meet you," Fill the Mind said as he took a step back and gave a quick wave. Then, both men turned about and headed back toward the road. They were soon marching down the path, away from the four travelers. It seemed to Prayerful that both of them were in an immediate discussion, venting their frustration over Steadfast's questioning.

Prayerful, Half-Heart, and Steadfast walked over to the campsite where Gentleness had everything ready for their morning meal. After prayer, they each took a plate and filled it with fruit and dried bread.

As they sat around eating, Half-Heart commented, "That was quite an interesting maneuver they showed us, wasn't it?"

"It is interesting … and dangerous," Steadfast said bluntly. "These men know nothing of real battle. If you were to try such a trick in an actual fight, you would end up with a broken wrist or arm."

"How do you know?" Half-Heart said condescendingly. "I am sure that these men know what they are talking about. After all, they *have* been highly trained."

"They are trained by men who lead people astray. The sad reality is that these men were taught to use the sword *contrary* to the King's design. I have heard of the Town of Academia before. It is filled with many people who look at God's truth like a man-made textbook and not the personal reality that it is. They desire to be teachers of the Law, but they don't really understand the basics of knowing the King. Honestly, these men probably only have a classroom knowledge of weaponry."

"So, no one in that town has actually fought in a real battle?" Prayerful asked.

"I am sure there are some, but most have not. A good number of the instructors completely deny that the sword was designed by the King. Thus, rather than relying upon the Lord's instructions of how to use it, they turn to their own flawed ideas. Sadly, such men tend to be held in high esteem as the greatest swordsmen, but in reality, they are just the opposite.... They are the pawns of Giant Liberalism whose castle lies just a few miles away."

Everyone momentarily stopped chewing their food and stared at Steadfast, shocked at what he had just revealed. It was appalling to think that such a place, which seemed so closely connected with good, was actually associated with the enemies of the King.

Steadfast continued, "There are a few there who will not go to that extreme. Such men do believe that the sword was designed by the King, and thus they rely upon its perfection, but the problem with them is that they only care to fill the mind."

"Isn't Academia not far from the Swamp of Self-Focus?" Gentleness asked.

Steadfast thought for a moment, "You know, I think you are right."

"I have heard that there are a number of people who have gotten lost in that bog," Gentleness explained. "What makes it even worse is that those who go there are often covered with the stinking Mud of Pride. I would imagine that many, if not all, from Academia have gone into that swamp at one point or another…. There are probably many still there today."

"Probably. And that leads to the other problem they have," Prayerful commented.

"What's that?" Half-Heart wondered.

"They seem to be so concentrated on knowledge and instruction that they forget what is most important: their heart. This is kinda what you were trying to point out, wasn't it, Steadfast?"

Steadfast nodded.

"What do you mean?" Half-Heart questioned. "I thought they seemed to be nice people…. They certainly were friendly."

"I am not talking about being friendly," Prayerful explained. "I am talking about loving God with all your heart. That should be the motivation for studying God's Word and knowing how to use His sword. Without a love for Him, you are just trying to impress others with your own skill."

"That is a good point," Steadfast interjected. "It seems to me that the way to Academia had once been traveled by many of the Pharisees who loved to receive the praise of men … and let's not forget what happened to them. Because of their pride, they rejected Christ, Himself."

"You see," Prayerful looked right into Half-Heart's eyes as he continued, "learning is certainly very good, and knowing God's truth is invaluable; in fact, I wish that more people would hide God's Word in their heart and be skillful with His sword. However, knowledge without a love for God is almost completely worthless."

"So, love for God should be what motivates us to dive into His truth," Half-Heart stated.

"Yes," Prayerful answered after he swallowed his

last bite, "but let me take it one step further. Love also will result in obedience. God's truth should impact our lives in every area. If we love Him, we will *keep* His commandments and not just *know* them."

Half-Heart simply stared off into the distance, nodding his head in understanding.

Self-Focus

The group traveled on in silent contemplation after their encounter with the men from Academia earlier that morning. Everyone was so focused on their prior conversation that they hardly noticed that the young wood which they had been walking through had gradually given way to a dense forest, blocking the view of the sky. A heavy layer of undergrowth gradually thickened to blanket the entire region and overshadow the pathway.

"It is hard to believe how blind those men are to their own issues," Half-Heart stated, interrupting everyone's thoughts. "I would never dream of disregarding the King's way of handling the sword."

Prayerful looked off into the forest and subtly rolled his eyes, remembering how Half-Heart had initially been enamored with the men from Academia. Once again, he was displaying his righteous talk while his actions spoke otherwise.

"They are proud, knowing nothing." Steadfast declared. "They dote over questions and strifes of words with only a classroom knowledge of how to handle the sword…. Things are quite different in a real battle."

"I have been in several skirmishes," Prayerful added. "However, I am certainly finding that there are many things I still have to learn. Something didn't seem right to me with their explanation, but I couldn't figure out what it was. "

"The more you learn the better you will be able to discern what not to do in a fight," Steadfast stated.

"Ha!" Half-Heart chuckled. "I am sure that any one of us could have beaten them!"

Prayerful and Steadfast shot each other a glance and had to suppress a laugh at Half-Heart's suggestion. The mere thought of Half-Heart in a duel against anyone who had a base understanding of swordsmanship was certainly humorous. Prayerful then began to wonder how he would have handled such a skirmish. Knowing that he could not figure out what was wrong with their swordsmanship, Prayerful figured that these two men were better trained than he was. Such a thought made his heart sink. *I certainly am not a good soldier*, he thought.

As they continued talking, Prayerful began to notice that the air was growing quite moist and thick. The smells of water plants began to fill the area, and he noticed moss hanging from the trees. Pushing through the undergrowth, they soon came out to the edge of a large, swampy region. Mirky water, with a few patches of dry ground, filled the land before them. Some of the trees grew on the dry ground along with various types of underbrush, while other trees were standing in the water itself. Although the swamp here appeared to be shallow, they all knew that travel would not be easy in this place. Making matters worse, no one realized that the aroma of the Me-First Plants had been dulling their spiritual senses for the last mile.

"I don't see any path at all through here,"

Gentleness declared while scanning the area before them.

"I am sure it won't be too hard to find. Maybe if we spread out, we can find it," Half-Heart stated confidently. "I'll wade over to that patch of higher ground over there," he offered, pointing slightly to their left.

"Good," Prayerful replied, "I will go straight ahead.... Maybe there will be a sign or a marker on one of those trees."

"Then I will go to the right since it looks more shallow over there," Steadfast stated.

"I don't know…" Gentleness said. "Something doesn't seem right.... I would think that the way would be more obvious. After all, the King constantly works to keep the way clear in the Forest of Daily Life. Wouldn't He want to keep the road clear and obvious all along the way?"

"I think you are worrying too much," Half-Heart replied. "We will find the path in no time."

After a slight pause, Gentleness replied, "Well, then … I think I will stay here until you find something definitive."

The three men stepped out into the knee-deep water, and their feet sank into the soft mud that lay underneath. Prayerful waded through the mirky water step after step, and soon arrived at the nearest tree which was standing in several feet of water. He slowly made his way around it, inspecting every inch for some sort of message. Finding none, he looked toward Steadfast and saw his friend searching for some sign of the roadway in the shallow areas of the swamp. Looking to his left, Prayerful noticed that Half-Heart was waist deep in the muddy water, progressing toward a patch of dry ground that he was going to examine.

With a sigh, Prayerful turned his attention back to the task at hand. He continued on from tree to tree, looking for some sort of a sign and studying the terrain for evidence of where a trail should go. After half an hour of fruitless searching, Prayerful grew more and more downcast and was beginning to wonder if he would ever find the way they should go. *I am certainly not very good at finding a trail*, he thought.

Prayerful waded over to a nearby patch of higher ground and climbed onto the dry grass. He called to Half-Heart and Steadfast, and within two minutes all three of them stood on this little island surrounded by the mirky waters of the swamp. The mud that cloaked their armor and clothing made them an even more pitiful sight than their downcast faces.

"I haven't found anything," Half-Heart stated immediately.

"Me, neither," Prayerful added, his chin and shoulders drooping slightly.

Steadfast merely shook his head.

"I think we should just cross the swamp and see if we can pick up the trail on the other side," Half-Heart quickly stated.

"I don't think that is wise. That is a good way to get lost," Steadfast rebutted. "Besides, I don't think it would be easy, or wise, to try to spend the night here."

"Well, do you have a better idea?" Half-Heart asked in frustration.

"I think if we travel along the edge of the swamp," Steadfast replied, "we will eventually find the other side of the trail.... Honestly, we would be less likely to miss it that way. Besides, by going along the edge of the swamp, we will be able to camp out on good dry ground without having to worry about getting covered in mud."

"But that would take too much time. This place looks huge," Half-Heart shot back as he swept his arm in a semicircle, to display the vastness of the swamp. "It would be much quicker to go across."

Prayerful listened to both of his friends, thinking that they each had some good ideas. As for himself, he figured he could not add much to the conversation, so he kept quiet.

Steadfast countered, "I have spent a good bit of time in the woods. I know how easy it is to get lost in such a place.... Trust me — we need to go around."

"Look," Half-Heart stated, "we don't want to waste too much time.... It would be much quicker to go across. We could go from one patch of dry ground to the next so we are not in the water the whole time. Besides, it seems to me that this would be the most likely way the trail would go."

Prayerful hated seeing his friends argue and wanted to stop them, but why should they listen to anything he had to say. After all, he was the one who had led them to this place.

"That is ridiculous," Steadfast replied in frustration. "That is exactly how you get lost, wandering aimlessly from one place to another. You will end up going in circles."

"You are not listening to me," Half-Heart retorted, raising his voice. "The path most likely follows the higher patches of dry ground.... It's obvious."

At that instant, someone burst into laughter off to their left. All three of them spun around and reached for their swords, not sure of who was there. About a dozen yards away, two men stood in the knee-deep water. The one whom they had heard had thrown his head back in laughter while his companion stood on the left with his eyes slightly lowered toward the ground as he chuckled and shook his head. Prayerful tried not to gawk at these strangers, but he found it difficult, for they were covered head to toe in a thick layer of mud that had obviously been caked on for a long time.

The man on the right declared, "You guys look like a mess. Don't you know how to take a bath?" At this remark, both strangers burst out in laughter once again.

"What about you?" Steadfast asked once they quieted down. "You guys are filthy!"

The man on the right spoke again, "There is nothing wrong with us.... We are fine.... Say, what are you guys doing here?"

"We are on our way to Near-to-God Mountain and kinda lost our trail around here. The road should be heading that way," Prayerful stated, pointing across the swamp.

"Well, we live here and have never seen any kind of trail like that..... There is a roadway that leads into this swamp, but there certainly isn't any that leads out on the other side," he stated with an air of indifference. "By the way, I am Arrogance, and this is False-Humility."

Prayerful was stunned and more confused than ever. *There is no road that leads out of here? That can't be,* he thought. *Certainly it must come out on the other side.* Before he could ask another question, Half-Heart said, "So you guys live here.... Why would you want to stay in such a place? There is hardly any dry ground ... and to get anywhere you have to wade through mud."

"It isn't that bad," False-Humility answered. "Besides, it is better than we deserve. After all, I am not very talented or smart. I often mess things up and fail at every turn. With how worthless I am, I don't deserve any better."

Arrogance quickly added, "For me, I like it better here than any other place I have been. I just can't stand other people … especially those who refuse to recognize my abilities."

"I see," Steadfast declared with a skeptical look.

"You don't believe me?" Arrogance questioned. "Well, let me tell you — I am very knowledgable about many things. I have attended some of the finest schools of the land and have learned under some of the greatest of teachers. Pick a topic … any topic, and I will show you how much I know, … and if you think I am wrong in any area, I will gladly challenge you to a battle of wits."

"Well," Prayerful said, a little disgusted with these men, "I don't think we have any questions for you.… I think we need to be on our way."

"All right, if that is what you wish," Arrogance declared with a hint of disappointment. After a moment of silence, he added, "If you are still looking for some kind of trail, you need to head over that way." Prayerful could clearly tell he was pointing back toward the spot where they had left Gentleness.

Prayerful was both dumbfounded and discouraged; he had completely lost the trail. He had failed. *I worked so hard to keep us on the right path, and now I have no idea where to go.*

With that, Prayerful turned, and with shoulders slumped, he waded back into the water. He trudged his way back to the trail as the word "failure" echoed in his mind. He did not bother to look behind him to see if the others would follow.… He did not care at this point.

After only a few steps, his foot caught on a hidden branch near the edge of one of the small islands, and he began to loose his balance. He tried to regain his footing, but in an instant he fell, face forward, and sunk

---

into a blanket of mud. Using his hands, he pushed himself up back out of the water and onto his knees as he gasped for air. After taking a few moments to catch his breath and clean his eyes and mouth, he was able to stand to his feet. As he stared at himself caked in mud, he could almost feel the gaze of the other men gawking at him.

Instantly, Arrogance and his friend burst into laughter once again. "You need to learn how to walk in this swamp," Arrogance shouted while his friend doubled over howling. "We haven't fallen like that in years. You poor simpleton!"

Underneath the layer of mud, Prayerful's cheeks grew red. He tried to fling the mud off his hands and wipe his face some more, but it did little to help his appearance. Frustrated and humiliated, he continued his trek back to the trail without looking behind him. Soon, he could hear the swishing of the mirky water behind him as his two friends followed him. He felt like the biggest fool ever.

Coming out from among the trees, they found Gentleness sitting among the grass on the bank reading her scroll of the Scriptures. Hearing them approach, she looked up, shock spreading across her face when she saw Prayerful. As they drew closer, she stood up and asked, "What happened?"

Half-Heart blurted out with a smirk on his face, "Prayerful decided to have a face-to-face meeting with the muddy floor of the swamp."

Prayerful avoided looking at anyone as he sank further into despair. "I am sorry. I got us into this mess, and now we have no idea where we should go."

"I am afraid that each one of you would have gotten lost in there," Gentleness calmly interjected. "Only a few minutes ago, I realized that this is the

Swamp of Self-Focus. You three have been wandering about in the Mud of Pride. No wonder you couldn't find the way!"

Prayerful glanced up at her as she continued, "We should not be here among the people who love themselves more than God.   Those who measure themselves by themselves are not wise. Besides, I could hear you guys arguing in there," Gentleness said, pointing toward the swamp. "It is only by pride that contention comes…. We need to turn around and get out of here, *now*!"

Her words struck a cord, and the three men lowered their heads in shame, knowing that she was right. Prayerful realized that when he was in despair, his thoughts were only on himself and never upon his King; he was consumed with a proud self-focus. The pride that filled the three of them made them into fools, for not only had they wasted time searching in vain, but now, they were a sweaty, muddy mess. Gentleness, however, figured out the problem because God resists the proud, but gives grace to the humble.

As they traced their footsteps back the way they had come, Prayerful tried to figure out what it was that caused them to end up in such a place. Eventually, it came to him: they had been so focused on themselves in their earlier conversation that they did not watch where they were going. It was not that they had lost the trail, but rather that they had wandered off onto another pathway. They should have kept their focus on their King.

After ten minutes of backtracking, they were able to find a clearing in the underbrush. The Road of Seeking ran right through the middle of it. They were pleasantly surprised to find a small, clear pool of water just off the side of the road. Within minutes, the three

men had completely washed themselves off, and they
then turned to each other, apologizing for their sin of
pride. It was a hard lesson to learn, but at least they
were back on the trail.

The Palace

Although this day was like any other day, Prayerful could sense a great weariness in himself and his companions that had not been there previously. Though they had seen distant villages and towns during the day, they had not found any place to spend the night for the past week and were forced to sleep on the hard earth. They all longed for a nicer place to lay their heads at night, but had not been successful in finding any suitable location. Not only that, but over the last few days, the Rains of Fatigue continued to soak them day and night, significantly slowing their progress and adding to their discouragement.

That morning, even though the rains had stopped and the sun had found its way from behind the clouds, they resumed their journey in solemn silence, thinking upon the dreariness of the last few days. Nothing noteworthy had happened since they left the swamp, but as they passed through the Fields of Forgetfulness, their minds gradually stopped dwelling on the goal of their journey. They instead began to think of how life was before they left on this journey, and, consequently, they began to long for the time when things would be easier. That afternoon, as they were passing near the Countryside of Fun, they were all wishing for some rest and relaxation — anything would do.

As the sun began to ease itself toward the western horizon, Prayerful's heart sank at the thought of another night in the outdoors. When they came around a turn in the road, a sign off to the left peaked their interest. It was pointing to a beautiful walkway which led over a nearby hill to their left. On it was written: "The Palace of Christian Relaxation — All are welcome."

Without any discussion, the friends unanimously decided to visit the Palace, hoping for a comfortable place to stay. They started down the pathway, and Prayerful's heart beat with excitement at the thought of a soft bed and a good night's rest. When they reached the top of the hill, a beautiful view lay before them. Flowering trees lined the walkway as it meandered down into a serene valley. At the base of the hill, a large, flat lawn lay, sprinkled with gardens and beautiful trees, enhancing the stunning structure at its center. The lawn, itself, looked like a gardener's dream, but the palace was even more impressive.

As they drew closer, Prayerful noticed that the four-story building was clearly built with beauty in mind. A round, flat-topped tower adorned either end of the magnificent structure as marble carvings decorated the exterior. Adding to the grandeur, gold and other precious stones beautified its facade in an amazing arrangement, obviously designed by a master craftsman. The beauty of the place radiated in the evening sun, whispering a welcome to all who passed by.

It did not take long for them to notice that all over the grassy expanse, small groups of people, dressed with the finest clothing, stood or sat around conversing. Some of them were even involved in various games or activities as their laughter reverberated throughout the valley.

As the four travelers approached the palace, a servant exited the main door and greeted them, "Welcome, friends. Are you looking to spend the night here?"

"We would love to, if that is all right," Prayerful said.

"Wonderful!" exclaimed the servant. "We enjoy having visitors. Come on in."

The servant led them through the massive oak doorway and into a grand, ornately decorated hall. At a quick glance, the guests could see that there were many rooms that came off this hallway. The high arched ceiling added to the beauty of the place and allowed everyone to see the balcony of the second floor. This high ceiling also permitted the enormous golden chandelier to illuminate the entire area.

The servant asked them to wait in the hall for a moment while he hurried into another room. Within a minute, he returned with a tall, muscular man; the servant introduced this large man as Mr. Take it Easy, the owner of the palace. The rest of the introductions were quickly made, and the servant took their traveling bags to the rooms where they would sleep.

After the servant left for the fourth floor, Take it Easy declared in a deep voice, "I am glad you decided to visit! Since I have a little time on my hands and it will be another half hour before supper, would you like me to show you around?"

"Yes, we would love that," Half-Heart said enthusiastically.

"Good, but let me first tell you a little of the history of this place — it will help you appreciate everything even more. The property here is quite old;

actually, some of our oldest records date back to the time of the apostles. My family has owned this land since that time, and we have always longed to invite Pilgrims in and give them a place to stay.

"My ancestors were wealthy and had originally built a hotel on this very spot, welcoming anyone who would come. They never had very large crowds, but they did enjoy what they were doing. It was a good time for them, but, sadly, as the years passed, fewer Pilgrims stopped by.

"As the hotel and property were passed down from generation to generation, the original buildings began to fall apart, and it seemed like we were on the verge of losing everything. That is why, upon inheriting the property, I decided to build a grand palace and expand the work that my family had begun. I had a great vision and was soon able to accomplish it because my aunt, Mrs. Prosperity, gave me a large portion in her inheritance. Ever since the construction was finished, I have been able to host a great number of Pilgrims as they serve the King."

"That is very generous of you," Gentleness commented.

"It is the least I can do for the King," Mr. Take it Easy said. "Well, let me show you around. This here, is the grand Hallway of Distraction," he declared as he waved his hand in a semicircle. "I am sure that you have already been able to enjoy its beauty, so let's move on." He then led them across the hall to the nearest room. "This is our chapel: Godly Appearance. Folks who come to the palace love our services; and our chaplain, Mr. Religious Talk, often has very interesting messages."

As Prayerful glanced around, he noted that the chapel was filled with the most luxurious seating he had ever seen. It looked so comfortable that he was sure many people could easily fall asleep during the sermon if they were not careful. In the front of the room, a large box sat on a table. This wooden coffer had a small hole cut in its top; it was the offering box named Send Someone Else. The beauty of the chapel caused Prayerful to want to stay longer in this room, but there was more to see.

Take it Easy then led them to another room that was full of the trinkets from Vanity. There were gizmos, household items, and clothing, along with jewelry, children's toys, and many other things. All these items were alluring to the eyes and had been placed on display in a very appealing way.

As he gazed around, this room made Prayerful a little uncomfortable, especially when he thought of the time he had been in the City of Vanity and the struggle he had had there with temptation. Take it Easy noticed his discomfort and said, "Although these things are from Vanity, they are not sinful in and of themselves. Don't worry — I merely allow these items in the Palace for the enjoyment of my guests."

Next, Take it Easy directed them to another room that was quite different from the others. It was shaped like a half-moon with all of the seats pointing toward the center of the far wall. Along that wall, stood a large stage, elevated three to four feet above the padded chairs. Prayerful figured that over two hundred people could sit comfortably in this room.

Take it Easy explained that this was where many would come to unwind and enjoy various plays. In fact, there were several shows every day. These plays typically came from Vanity and had been known to be popular among those who attended the arena in that city. Take it Easy, once again, emphasized that he did not allow anything bad to be presented at the palace; only good, moral stories were allowed. Prayerful secretly wondered, *What is his standard for choosing which plays are good, and which ones are not?* He did not get a chance to ask, for Take It Easy ushered them to their next stop, continuing their tour.

The last room that they visited was the art room. The first thing that Prayerful noticed was the King's armor displayed on the back wall. As he gazed about the room, Prayerful was amazed to behold the great variety of artwork. There were many paintings portraying various scenes in the Bible, and some verses of encouragement were also hung on the walls. They were informed that Scriptural passages of warning or judgment were typically not displayed since Take It Easy wanted to uplift, not discourage, all who come.

The other pictures in the room presented the grandeur of Vanity and its activities. Prayerful found it odd that there was not a single picture that showed Vanity in a negative light, but instead, they tended to show various activities of that city and even honored some of Vanity's celebrities. As he stood observing the room, Prayerful also found it odd that the pictures of Vanity seemed to be subtly crowding out the pictures from the Bible. While gazing at the artwork, another thought came to Prayerful's mind: *No man can serve two masters.*

At that moment, a servant entered the room, announcing that dinner was served. Prayerful continued pondering these things as Take It Easy led them to a sizable dining hall which was as beautifully decorated as the rest of the building. Six colossal wooden tables filled the room, making it possible to feed a great number of people. Centerpieces adorned the ornate tablecloths, adding a wonderful beauty to the silverware and water glasses which were placed by each seat.

Several dozen guests were already present and stood around, conversing in groups of three to six people. Shortly, all of the other guests arrived and were shown their seats by the six servants who were designated to keep everything running smoothly. After everyone was seated, Mr. Take it Easy led the gathering in prayer for the food. Then, the meal was served.

As they ate, Prayerful thought that he had not experienced such a fancy meal in all of his life. He watched as the servants continuously brought out plates of food, delivering them to the guests during this five-course dinner. He was a little nervous and struggled to relax because he was sure that he did not know all of the fine points of etiquette; however, he kept watching other people to make sure he did things right.

The four friends were sitting near the end of their table, not too far away from where their host was seated. Steadfast and Gentleness sat across from Prayerful and Half-Heart. Prayerful quickly introduced himself and his friends to the others sitting nearby. To Prayerful's left sat Not-on Fire while Love of Stuff sat on Half-Heart's right. Carnality and Self-Pleasing were on either side of Gentleness and Steadfast. Not-on Fire seemed to be a well-refined gentleman, both in his fancy clothing and in the way he presented himself. They chatted for a while and were even able to share a little of their own stories.

After receiving the second course of their meal, Prayerful turned to Not-on Fire and said, "You mentioned that when you left the town of World Desire, you were trying to get to Near-to-God Mountain and that you only stopped here because you were tired. When do you plan on resuming your journey?"

Not-on Fire was a little taken aback by this question and very clumsily set his water glass down on the table, spilling some of its contents. "I don't know. I still would like to get there someday," he stated as he wiped his mouth with the napkin, "but I don't think I am quite ready to go."

"What do you have left to do to get ready?" Prayerful questioned.

"Well, I guess it is more that I have a list of things that I still want to do before I leave. This Palace is a fascinating place, full of many surprises," he exclaimed as he picked up his fork laden with food. Not-on Fire then let out a loud burp and stated, "I am especially wanting to see the latest show from Vanity: *Worldly Pull.*" As he was bringing the food to his mouth, the gravy-covered veal on his fork accidentally slipped off the utensil, rolled down his white shirt, and landed in his lap. Prayerful stifled a smile, glad that it had not happened to him.

After Not-on Fire cleaned up the mess, Prayerful asked, "Do you think that all of the exciting things here will make you want to stay longer and delay your journey even more?"

"I suppose so; but I am not in a rush to leave. I like it here a lot. Just wait, the more you see of this place, the more you will like it," Not-on Fire said with a smile.

Prayerful was puzzled over this man's attitude. He could not understand why someone would basically ignore the pilgrimage he was called to make. He was just about to ask something else, but Not-on Fire quickly turned to Carnality and began speaking to her, apparently uncomfortable with Prayerful's questions. This man certainly was not all that he appeared to be — both in manners and in his heart for God.

Prayerful's mind wandered off for a minute as he continued to think about his conversation with Not-on Fire. His mind snapped back to the discussion at the table when he heard Half-Heart asking Self-Pleasing, "What is the best thing about staying here at the Palace?"

"Well, that is hard to say," Self-Pleasing responded in a slow, strange accent. "There are many things that I like about this place. Probably the best thing is that Mr. Take it Easy gives us free access to his treasury." Evidently sensing doubt in Half-Heart, he added, "If you don't believe me, look around and see how well people are dressed. Everyone here is given money, and many will spend hours shopping in the nearby village of Greed. We don't have to worry about anything."

After a slight pause, Self-Pleasing continued, "I guess the other thing that I love about this place is that we have a lot of entertainment and fun. Many people who stay here own the latest gadgets from Vanity.... No one can accuse us of not being up with the times," he said with a chuckle. "Don't worry — Take it Easy is always careful that everything around here is morally ok."

Steadfast, who by now had been drawn into the conversation, interjected a question, "What about the King? What do you do for Him?"

"Good question," Self-Pleasing commented. "I am glad that you brought it up. God is certainly very important to us. When you came here, were you shown the chapel?" he asked. Prayerful and his friends nodded. "Ok, well, on Sundays, even though there are some who would rather sleep in or do some activity, we have a good crowd in the chapel. We love to come, sing, and hear Mr. Religious Talk as he preaches. You see,

God's truth is something we love to learn. Also, since we want others to know of Christ, we send offerings to help various people all over the world proclaim the truth of the King.

"There are many other activities that we do for the Lord," he continued. "We often have fellowships and activities together. We try to encourage each other and dwell on the wonderful promises from Scripture.... As I think of it, I would say that we have need of nothing here."

Prayerful gazed off into the distance as he tried to soak in all they had seen and had been told. This Palace certainly was quite a place of beauty, entertainment, and riches. On top of it all, the people even spoke openly and eagerly of the Lord. Prayerful thought, *No wonder so many people like it here;* but he could tell something was amiss.

Escape by Night

Prayerful paced back and forth in his room, trying to unravel his thoughts about this Palace. After supper, they had spent some time talking with various other guests. Everyone certainly seemed friendly, and they even encouraged him to join in some of the activities. Although he longed to indulge in all the things that were offered, a voice inside him whispered, "Seek those things which are above." At that moment, an uneasiness in his heart had begun to grow; something was definitely wrong, but he was not sure what. Although he was tempted to ignore the warning, he did not.

After everyone retired to their own room for the night, Prayerful found room number 40 where he was to stay, entered, and then shut the door and lit his lamp. He needed time to sort everything out and was afraid that the darkness would pull him to sleep. The guests here seemed to be wonderful people, for Prayerful had many good conversations with those who spoke deeply of the truths of the King and the wonders of the Celestial City; however, despite being good, these people lacked something that Prayerful could not put his finger on.

As he paced back and forth, a thought suddenly hit him: in the Art Room, there were no pictures of warning or judgment. Thinking further, he also realized that everyone in the Palace was focused on the positive aspects of truth. Some of the people had talked about their joy of being rescued from sin, but otherwise, everyone seemed to care *only* about things that were uplifting. *Do they ever think about the warnings given in Scripture? ... Do they seek to warn the world of the wrath to come?* Thinking further, he added: *What about themselves ... are they concerned about laying up treasure in heaven rather than on earth?*

He walked over to the window, barely noticing the blackness of the night as his mind shifted to his conversation with Not-on Fire. How could a man, at one point in life, long for Near-to-God Mountain, then get to the place where he has no drive to get there? It seemed to Prayerful that this man's attitude changed while he had been here at the Palace of Christian Relaxation. Something about this place, itself, was just not right, for it actually hindered Pilgrims in their journey — hence, the large crowd.

At that moment, something caught his eye. On the nearby end table, an ornate vase full of flowers sat in a grand display of beauty, enticing his eyes to behold its wonder. He knew that this vase was a very coveted item called Earthly Value. As he went over to inspect its golden elegance, he was a little surprised to find that the carnations were fake — he had imagined that such a palace as this would only use real flowers. Upon closer examination, he also found that the vase itself was a cheap decoration of painted wood. He was stunned; what appeared to cost many gold coins was barely worth a loaf of bread. *I wonder how many other things around here are not as precious as they seem to be?*

In that instant, Prayerful snapped to attention, his heart racing; he had heard something. Though it was a faint, indiscernible sound, it sent a strange fear through his heart. It sounded like pieces of metal clinking together. Prayerful tried to relax and convince himself that it was probably a servant somewhere in the Palace, but the feeling of foreboding did not leave him.

Prayerful turned out his light and tiptoed through the darkness over to the door. Placing his right ear against the wooden frame, he listened for a minute but heard nothing. *I must be getting jumpy,* he thought. Figuring that it was just his imagination, he was about to go back over to re-light the lamp when the noise, once again, quietly echoed throughout the building. Playing the noise over again in his mind, he realized that it sounded like someone was walking around in a suit of armor. Prayerful's heart raced even faster as his mind flashed back to the battles he had faced with Believer; his instincts knew there was trouble.

Prayerful girded on his sword in the darkness of his room, and then stumbled back to the door. He reached his hand down, found the doorknob, and slowly began to turn it. Much to Prayerful's relief, the latch did not make any noise. With his right hand on the hilt of his sword, he opened the door a crack and peered out into the hallway.

A dim light in the distance illuminated the area just enough for him to see as he looked up and down the corridor. As far as he could tell, the coast was clear. He was about to shut the door again when he faintly heard a squeaky door in the distance move on its hinges. Although such noises could easily be excused as a normal occurrence, he followed his instincts and continued to assume that there was danger.

Prayerful slowly opened the door further,

checked both ways in the hall, and then slipped out of his room. He heard a faint scrape of metal against stone, coming from the stairway to the lower levels. He made his way over there, carefully placing every step so as not to make a single squeak in the floor.

At the top of the steps, he listened some more. The clinking had stopped and was replaced by faint whispering. He figured that there were at least two people talking — maybe more. The words were unintelligible, so he carefully went down the steps to the third floor. When he made it to the bottom step, it seemed to Prayerful that the whispering was echoing from the great hallway on the first level.

As he made his way to the next set of stairs leading down to the second floor, the whispering stopped and Prayerful could hear footsteps walking away. He was about to retreat back to the fourth floor when he heard another door shut below. He waited a little longer and soon heard the door open again and the footsteps returning. Within moments, the men below resumed their conversation.

Prayerful quickly made his way to the head of the stairs leading to the second floor so he could listen. Here he could make out bits and pieces of the conversation.

"I … keys, just … asked," the first voice stated.

"Good," a familiar, yet somewhat dark, voice responded. Sensing that this conversation could be important, Prayerful cautiously crept down the next set of steps and strained his ears to pick up every word.

The dark voice continued, "Fools … once morning comes … They spent a good bit … about the King and … that they still want to go on."

Prayerful finally reached the bottom of the steps and peered between the rungs of the balcony railing.

He was stunned when he saw the man who was speaking — it was Take it Easy. Here, Prayerful was able to clearly catch the end of the conversation.

"I tried to lure them into the attractions here, but that didn't work." The evil voice whispered. "We will try harder tomorrow."

"Then why did you want these, Lord Apathy?" the other man said as he lifted a large ring filled with keys.

Once again, Prayerful was shocked, for, in that instant, he recognized that Take it Easy was none other than the infamous Lord Apathy. Realization that this whole Palace was a giant trap hit him like a thunderbolt. Prayerful felt like a hunted animal that was caught in the lion's den, and he wished he could melt into the wall.

"I need to make sure that those newcomers stay here till the morning," Apathy continued. "*Then*, I can get them consumed with the cares and riches of the world. They need to learn to … *enjoy* themselves," he said with a sadistic chuckle.

"So, then, you want me to use the Locks of Earthly Love to keep them in their rooms," the other man said.

"Yes, but wait," Lord Apathy commanded. "I want to make sure they are well asleep first. If they hear you, then our task will be … more difficult. If worse comes to worse and they insist on continuing their journey, I will have to use the Poison of Indulgence."

"Ok. So, should I give them another half hour?" the other man asked as he slightly lifted the keys.

"That will be fine. We will keep our guards posted through tomorrow evening in case they try to get away, but that should give me plenty of time to take care of them."

Prayerful watched as the two men exited through different doors and was relieved that neither one came to the stairs. His heart pounded, and he wanted to scream, knowing that he did not have much time to get everyone out of here. Quickly bowing his head, he prayed, "Deliver me not over unto the will of mine enemies."

He quietly hurried back to the fourth floor, hoping that it would not be hard to wake his friends. Going first to Steadfast and Gentleness's door, he tapped on it and waited a few seconds, but there was no answer. He then knocked a little louder, hoping no one else would hear him. The shuffling of feet in the room brought a small measure of relief to Prayerful's trembling heart.

Steadfast opened the door and said, "What is wrong?" Prayerful was shocked to see that his friend was fully dressed and armed.

"I just found out that this place is a trap of the enemy! In less than half an hour, they are going to lock us in our rooms to make sure we don't escape."

A knowing look crossed Steadfast's face. "We suspected something was wrong, and we were still talking about it," he responded. "We'll get ready."

"I will get Half-Heart," Prayerful volunteered.

"Good."

Steadfast closed the door, and Prayerful tiptoed across the hallway to another room. He, once again, tapped the door, waited a few moments, and then knocked. There was no answer. He tried several more times but did not have any success. After several minutes, Prayerful was getting close to a panic; he had no idea how much time had passed, and he knew that they could get caught at any moment. His heart was beating wildly, and his palms were sweating. He did not know what to do.

Prayerful nearly jumped out of his skin when he heard another door open. He spun around, hand on his sword, but was relieved when he saw Steadfast and Gentleness emerging from their room.

"I can't wake him!" Prayerful whispered when Steadfast came closer.

"Did you try the door?"

Prayerful looked down, grabbed the handle, and found that it turned freely. Feeling a little foolish, he pushed the door open a few inches and heard the heavy breathing of their friend.

"I will get him," Steadfast declared. "You gather your belongings."

"Good idea," Prayerful answered, knowing they did not have much time. He tiptoed back over to his room, entered, and re-packed his bag in the dimness of the night. It took him some time, but soon, he had his armor completely on and his bag over his shoulder. He left the room and silently shut the Door of Earthly Affection behind him.

Gentleness was standing at the head of the stairway, watching for anyone who would come. She gave Prayerful the signal that the coast was still clear. Prayerful stole across the hallway again to Half-Heart's open door. When he entered the room, he could smell the moist outdoor air; Half-Heart had evidently opened a window before he went to bed.

Prayerful could barely discern Half-Heart sitting on his bed with his head in his hands. The man seemed half asleep and was clearly reluctant to get up. Prayerful could also make out Steadfast moving about in the dark, collecting his friend's belongings and shoving them into the bag. Things were taking too long for Prayerful, but he did his best to be patient. Once the bag was packed, Prayerful grabbed it from Steadfast and threw the over-laden pack over his own shoulder, knowing that Half-Heart would likely drop it.

Steadfast had to help Half-Heart to his feet. *He must be really out of it*, Prayerful said to himself and began to wonder how they could escape with him. Steadfast put his arm around Half-Heart and walked him over to the door. Prayerful followed them out into the hallway, and after shutting the door to Half-Heart's room, they moved over to the steps. Progress was far too slow, but they soon made it to the stairway. Turning around one last time, Prayerful double-checked that all the doors were closed; he was hoping that, as long as they did not get caught in their escape, their absence would not be noticed until morning. Maybe they could sneak out a kitchen door or something.

They slowly moved down to the third floor with Prayerful in the lead. When they arrived on the second floor, Prayerful looked over the balcony into the Hallway of Distraction to see if the coast was clear. His throbbing heart sank when he saw that the main door of the palace was guarded by two, fully armed men, and thus they could not even make it down to the first floor without being spotted. If they tried to rush the door, the ruckus of a fight would certainly bring more trouble. They were trapped.

In the softest whisper he could make, Prayerful explained the situation to Steadfast. In hushed tones, they tried to come up with a plan when another noise struck terror into their hearts. A door on the first level had just opened. Prayerful froze as he peeked through the spindles of the banister and saw the man with the keys emerge from a room below. He was heading toward the stairs with purpose in his step — the half hour was up.

Prayerful made a frantic motion to his friends, and they understood immediately what was happening. They could not go forward, and they dare not go back up the steps out of fear of being caught. No one knew what to do as they stared at each other in shocked silence for a few agonizingly long moments.

Eventually, Gentleness, with urgency in her motions, pointed to two large bushes beyond the edge of the steps. Immediately, everyone knew what she was thinking. They quietly hurried over to the shrubbery, hoping there would be adequate cover for a hiding place. Steadfast practically dragged Half-Heart behind one leafy bush while Gentleness and Prayerful hid behind the other. The footsteps of their adversary grew closer, causing the four of them to freeze in position.

As Prayerful looked between the leaves of the large plant, he saw not one, but three, men ascend the stairs. The one in the lead, who had been talking to Apathy earlier, had a set of keys and was now fully armed. The other two, carrying poleaxes, were apparently coming along in case there was trouble. Prayerful held his breath as these men went to the next set of steps and began to ascend them.

Prayerful suddenly realized something: the man with the keys was the very servant who welcomed them to the Palace. Prayerful's eyes were opened now to who he was; he was Apathy's right hand man: Worldly Draw. Later, he discovered that the other two minions were Ignorance and Sightless.

When the three henchmen were out of view, Prayerful took a quick sigh of relief, and then he and Gentleness snuck over to Steadfast and Half-Heart. "We need to get as far away from these steps as possible," Prayerful whispered. "We don't know how quickly they will be back."

"Since we can't go up or down, let us move toward the back side of the Palace," Steadfast replied. "It may be safer there, away from the guards at the front door."

Not having time to develop more of a plan, they silently crept along the dim walkway toward the rear of the building. Prayerful knew this maneuver was risky, but it was the only one they could come up with. They reached the far end of the hall and were thankful that they were a good ways away from both the stairs and the guards at the front door.

Just as they were surveying the area, trying to figure out their next step, they heard footsteps coming from the floor above. Looking around, they could not find any place to hide. They began to wish that they had stayed behind the bushes, but they knew it was too late to go back. They did the only thing they could do and went to the far corner of the balcony, next to the window where it was darkest, and hid in the shadows.

The four of them waited, with their backs pressed against the wall, for several unbearable moments. Soon, they saw the feet of the three henchmen descending the stairs. Prayerful could feel every beat of his heart as his hands grew sweaty. He watched in horror while the three men came all the way down the stairs, convinced he and his comrades would be discovered. To his relief, the three workers of evil did not even look up as they walked around to the next flight of steps and descended to the first floor. He breathed a small sigh of relief but knew that they were still in danger.

They all huddled in a tight group to whisper and discuss their plan. Thankfully, Half-Heart, by now, was more alert and aware of the danger they were in. Looking at the window, Prayerful thought, *God has provided a way of escape,* as an idea came to him. He whispered his plan to the others and they liked it. Even though they could not go out any door, they could use Steadfast's rope and escape out the window.

Quickly, Steadfast pulled the Rope of Spiritual Fervor out of his bag and uncoiled it. After a minute, he found the middle of the rope and tied a special knot to the banister, next to one of the spindles. The one half of the rope was secure and would be what they would use to climb down. The other half, when pulled, would release the slip knot so that the entire rope could be retrieved. While Steadfast was working at the knot, Half-Heart quietly opened the window. They then eased the rope down the outside wall, being careful not to let it make any noise.

Steadfast went out the window and down the rope first to make sure the ground was clear and there were no guards. After a full minute, he pulled on the rope twice to signal "all clear." Gentleness then eased her way out of the window and silently reached the ground. Next, Half-Heart climbed out and began working his way down. When he was about seven feet off the ground, his hands slipped on the rope, and he began to fall, unable to slow himself down. He hit the ground with a thud, and Prayerful recognized that he needed to hurry in case Half-Heart's crash landing had been heard.

Within several seconds, Prayerful climbed out the window, held the rope in one hand, and closed the window as far as he could with the other. He quickly slid down. When he reached the bottom, he began pulling on the other side of the rope to undo the slip knot. When all of the rope was on the ground, Steadfast began to wind it as quickly as possible. That is when trouble came.

Around the far edge of the one tower, a torch came into view, followed by another. Their escape had been noticed, and Prayerful's heart sank once again. Steadfast threw the rope into his bag and motioned for everyone to follow him. They ran twenty yards to a large flower garden and ducked down behind the tallest of the plants. Steadfast glanced behind them and noticed that the guards were slowly surveying the back wall of the palace — they had not been spotted yet. Keeping low to the ground, the four friends worked their way to the other side of the garden, hoping they could make their way to another hiding spot farther away.

Once they got to the far side of the garden, they were a little relieved to see the forest about one hundred yards away. If they could get there, it would be much easier to hide among the trees and sneak out of this valley. Steadfast peered through the bushes to see where the guards were. Then, he snuck over to Prayerful and reported, "They are still examining the back of the Palace. If we move now and keep this garden between them and us, we should make it."

"Ok, let's go," Prayerful announced.

They all quietly jogged across the flat lawn, being careful not to be seen and doing their best to keep their armor from clanking. Only then did Prayerful notice that a strange, heavy fog was falling over the entire region and had already engulfed the upper half of the Palace. Prayerful knew that if the fog settled on the ground, it could make things difficult for their pursuers to locate them, but it could also make things harder for them to find their way back to the main road. Despite his concern, he decided to take things one step at a time.

They reached the trees without incident and as quietly as possible, entered the woods. Prayerful turned around to talk to his friends, hoping to come up with their next step, but when he did, what little relief he felt was dashed. The two men with torches were coming across the lawn and would be upon them within a minute.

Prayerful turned to the right and led the group in a direction parallel to the Palace. They remained far enough into the woods to remain somewhat hidden while carefully keeping an eye on the guards of Worldly Love. Continuing on in silence, they soon noticed that the men with torches were scanning the ground, clearly searching for something. *They are tracking us!* Prayerful realized. They had to keep on moving.

Just then, several more men carrying torches emerged from the tower and joined the search party. Prayerful picked up the speed, knowing they needed to get out of here fast. They made their way along the edge of the woods and were soon climbing the hill adjacent to the Palace, but they were still being followed.

Prayerful continued to press on, eager to get out of the area, but just as they crested the hill, a twig snapped a few yards to their left. Dropping to the ground, everyone held his breath, hoping they had not been seen.

"Good Pilgrims, come this way," a voice called out in an urgent whisper.

They remained silent for fear that this was a trap. In the darkness, Prayerful saw movement a few feet from him, and he completely froze. At that moment, a man came out from behind a tree and knelt down, putting a gentle hand on Prayerful's shoulder. He said, "Don't be afraid. I am Prudent, servant of the King. You must follow me further into the woods to get away from these evil men."

Prudent stood up and began walking deeper into the forest. Somehow, Prayerful knew that this man could be trusted. He quietly stood back up, and his friends imitated his example. They then began following this stranger deeper into the woods and away from their pursuers — and the Palace.

They continued on for a half-hour and eventually crossed the stream of Resolve, leaving the fog behind them. Soon, they were in an open, moonlit field, and the fear of the evening began to fade away. Cautiously, they made their way to the other side of the meadow and were back on the Road of Seeking.

Prudent led them down the road, and after another half hour, they spotted a lone, impenetrable tower resting upon a large hill. Within a few minutes, they were at the base of this structure, and their guide led them to a door, inviting them in. They were at the Tower of Remembrance.

A Time to Remember

In the dimness of the moonlit night, Prayerful entered through the door of the tower and found himself in a small room. He crept along so as not to run into anything, and his three friends followed close behind. They waited inside the tower while Prudent remained just outside the door to make sure they had not been followed. After fifteen minutes, Prudent entered declaring, "All clear." Everyone took a sigh of relief.

Prudent found his way to a nearby table and lit a candle. Then, after barring the door, he escorted the group into another room. In the soft glow of the candle's flickering flame, Prayerful quickly observed that this new room was the kitchen. It certainly was not large, but it was not cramped either.

Prudent added a few pieces of firewood to the hot coals in the hearth, and soon a warm, crackling fire was licking away at the dry wood. As the room became more illuminated, Prayerful noted that shelves, loaded with various spices and ingredients, lined one wall while an assortment of pots, pans, and cooking utensils hung from another. Next to the far wall stood a table with six chairs.

Prudent invited everyone to take a seat while he retrieved a loaf of bread from a nearby shelf and brought it to the table with a cutting knife. As he began to slice the bread, he inquired of their journey. Prayerful explained their adventures while Prudent listened and worked. After cutting several slices and pouring water for everyone, Prudent finally sat down to hear the rest of their story.

"I wish we had realized the dangers of The Palace of Christian Relaxation, but I guess we let our guard down because we were so worn out," Prayerful stated as he finished telling the account of their journey.

"Yes," Prudent replied. "It is certainly good and important to have rest.   However, such things as are promoted in the Palace, innocent as they may seem, can be used as bait to pull us off the path of the King and suck us into the ways of the world. We must be careful with such things that they do not distract us from what is truly important…. That is exactly what happens there.

"You are not the first to have fallen for that trap, and I am sorry to say that you won't be the last. I have been able to help some escape from that awful place, but most who go there have no desire to leave."

"Because they enjoy themselves too much?" questioned Gentleness.

"Yes, and because they are inflicted with the Poison of Indulgence."

"Tell me," Prayerful interjected, "how did you know we were trying to escape and where to find us?"

"Helping people escape is part of the job that the King has given me. From the top of this tower, I can see great distances; thus, I am able to observe those heading toward danger. Yesterday, I saw you as you came along the road toward the Palace. Knowing that most people see the sign and fall for the trap, I left the tower as quickly as possible and ran to stop you, but I was too late. By the time I got there, you had already entered through the doors. Unfortunately, this almost always happens — very few have their guard up.

"I hid in the woods around the palace, and using my pocket telescope, I kept an eye on you through the windows. After dusk fell and everyone retired to their rooms, I knew the hour of decision would come. You would either choose to stay or realize the danger and try to leave. As I waited, I did grow a little nervous when I saw the fog fall on the area."

"Were you afraid that the fog would make it too difficult to see our movements?" Half-Heart questioned.

"No. The problem is that the fog is actually from the Enchanted Grounds. It lulls every Pilgrim in its path to sleep and dulls their spiritual senses. Over the years, this evil mist has been expanding its influence, and by now, it has gone so far that it easily reaches the Palace. Consequently, there are many that are walking about in a spiritual daze, never desiring to continue their pilgrimage.

"Anyway," Prudent continued with his story, "once you lit the lamp, Prayerful, I knew that it was only a matter of time before you would understand what was really happening there. You see, the Lantern of Truth exposes the emptiness of the things in that Palace." In a flash, Prayerful remembered the vase and realized that it was the lantern that helped him see it was fake.

"Knowing that the front of the building would be guarded heavily, I guessed you would escape out the back and then head for the woods. Figuring that you wanted to continue on the Road of Seeking, I hid in the forest on the northeastern side of the house…. And that is where I met you."

"I am glad that the Lord sent you along to help us," Steadfast stated as Prayerful nodded his agreement.

"He will always provide a way of escape and will help you as you seek after Him," Prudent replied. "If you search for Him with all your heart, you will find him."

They continued talking for a little while longer, but soon the excitement of their escape wore away, and the lateness of the hour caused dreariness to fall upon them all. Prudent led them to several guest chambers where they each found a welcoming, comfortable bed and were finally able to have a peaceful rest.

*　　*　　*

Around the breakfast table in the morning, they all benefited from Prudent's conversation and encouragement. After they were all finished eating and were satisfied, Prudent offered to show them the great wonder of the tower. Everyone was excited and readily accepted the idea.

They followed Prudent through the doorway and into a room with a stone, spiral staircase. He led them up the steps in silence for a little while as they enjoyed the cool dampness of the tower.

Before they reached the top, Prudent said, "When the children of Israel fled from the bondage of Egypt, they came to the Red Sea and were soon trapped with Pharaoh's army behind them and the sea before them. They were so terrified that they began to accuse Moses of trying to kill them and declared it would have been better if they had stayed in Egypt as slaves. Here is the question: Why didn't they have to fear?"

"Because God was delivering them," Prayerful answered. "He had just shown His power through the plagues that had been poured out on Egypt."

"That is right. They forgot His power very quickly," Prudent replied as he continued to lead them up the stairway. "We have a natural tendency to forget the things that God has done for us."

At this moment, Prudent stopped at the top of the steps to unlatch a large wooden door. As he opened it, Prayerful was temporarily blinded by the morning sun shining through the doorway. They stepped out into the fresh air, and Prayerful had to wait for a few moments for his eyes to adjust to the brightness of the outdoors.

Once he was accustomed to the light, Prayerful observed that they were on top of the round tower. The structure was approximately fifty feet across. Around the edge of the tower, a six-foot-high stone wall had been built. This battlement had rectangular gaps every ten feet in case the tower came under attack and its defenders needed to shoot at the enemy.

Prayerful walked over to the nearest of these gaps and took a moment to look down to the ground below. From what he could tell, the tower was about forty feet tall, and its situation on top of a large hill gave it the ideal location to see far into the distance.

He took a few moments to gaze at the beautiful scene before him. The forests and fields seemed to stretch for miles in all directions. Occasionally, he would spot a farm or even a town, but as he gazed way off into the distance, specific objects grew less distinguishable until they faded completely away into the land beyond.

Turning around, he saw Prudent striding over to the large platform that sat in the middle of the tower. This twenty-foot-wide circular structure was elevated five feet above the tower's roof, and in the middle of this platform, a fifteen-foot-long telescope rested on a cone-shaped wooden stand.   Prayerful watched as Prudent came up to the enormous instrument and gazed through its eyepiece.

"I would like everyone to come up here," Prudent announced.

While they were climbing the steps to the platform, he began to make some adjustments with one of the two wheels that were near the balancing point of the scope.   Once the adjustments were made, he returned to the eyepiece and smiled in satisfaction.

"The children of Israel forgot what God had done for them, and they consequently fell into despair. Many Pilgrims forget how God has led them in the past, and thus many tend to wander astray. The King built this tower mainly as a place for Pilgrims to look back and remember where they have been.   This is the great Reminiscing Telescope," he announced as he waived his hand toward the large instrument.

"Now," he continued, "I can only have one person look through at a time, so you will have to take turns. Half-Heart, you will be first. Come, and tell us what you see."

Half-Heart approached the eyepiece, bent down a few inches, and looked through the lens. "I see the Palace of Christian Relaxation," he commented. "There are a good number of people enjoying themselves outside, and it looks like one group is playing some sort of game."

"Ok," Prudent stated.   "Look away from the palace into the woods behind it."

"Umm … I don't really see anything," Half-Heart stammered.

For the next several minutes, Prudent coaxed him as to where he should look, but Half-Heart insisted that nothing was there. After a while of fruitless search, he completely gave up and allowed Steadfast to have a turn.

When Steadfast gazed at the forest behind the palace, he immediately exclaimed, "I think I see something. It looks like a rooftop. Wait … I think I can see the outline of the entire building. It seems to be purposefully concealed … but it is definitely there."

After Gentleness and Prayerful had their turn examining the structure, Half-Heart turned down a second opportunity to look; he would simply take their word for it. Prudent then explained, "That palace was built from the stones of Laodicea. Although everyone thinks it is a wonderful place, they don't realize that it is actually the Fortress of Lukewarmness. The other building that you saw is one of the three unknown secrets of that stronghold."

Taking a slight breath, he continued, "As people are drawn by Apathy's luxurious palace, they do not realize the danger they are stepping into. Pilgrims on their journey often get weary and lose sight of their true goal; thus, they readily accept his invitation. Although there is certainly a proper time for rest, the problem is that these people begin seeking their own pleasure and turn their focus off of Christ. Lord Apathy will give them the things they want, and, slowly, he poisons them so that they long for the wealth and prosperity of the world, forgetting their love for God.

"Over time, these people begin serving Lord Apathy and eventually are cast into his Prison of Spiritual Poverty. They remain there in scant rags, serving in his Workhouse of Misery and Blindness. The sad reality is that they are so intoxicated by Apathy's poison that they continually imagine that they are rich and increased with goods."

Prayerful shuttered as Gentleness voiced what he was thinking, "And we were almost trapped there.... I can hardly believe it!... It is so odd that such a beautiful palace is actually a horrible prison."

"Yes, you are right. I find that, often, when you look back to where you have been, you can see things more clearly; but sometimes, it is just too late. By realizing the danger and choosing to leave, you have escaped much suffering." After a slight pause, Prudent stated, "Let's move on to something else."

Prudent walked back over to the large knobs at the center of the telescope and began to make some more adjustments. Within several minutes, the large instrument was rotated ninety degrees to the north and was aimed higher up into the mountains. After turning several other small knobs near the eyepiece, he was ready for them to see the next sight.

Gentleness had the first opportunity to look through the telescope this time. She did not speak for several minutes, and she had a very somber look on her face as she gazed through the great instrument. Prayerful could not tell what she was thinking, but he knew that she was looking at something very important. When she eventually stood up, she silently turned away and wiped a tear from her eye.

Steadfast, too, had his turn to gaze through the scope, and he, as well, remained silent. When his turn was over, he gazed off into the distance with the most solemn and sorrowful expression that Prayerful had ever seen. Prudent did not press either of them for answers but let them meditate in silence.

Half-Heart had a similar reaction though not quite as strong as the others. Whatever it was, it did leave a profound impression on him, despite the fact that he did not gaze long at the object. Prayerful knew that whatever they saw was something very important, and he prepared his heart for what he might observe.

When Prayerful looked through the eyepiece, the sight before him brought a great variety of emotions. Sorrow and shame mixed with joy and wonder as he beheld a sight that he had gazed at once before. The telescope was zoomed in on a lonely hill where stood an old rugged cross. Through the scope, he could still make out the stains on the wood where the blood of the spotless Lamb of God had been shed when Christ took on himself the sin of the world, paying its penalty.

In a flash, Prayerful's mind took him back to the time that he had stood at the foot of that very cross, beholding its wonder. Although he willingly admitted his sin, and thus was rejected by his earthly father, the heavenly Father had forgiven him of that sin and welcomed him as a son. All of this was possible because of what Christ had done on the cross. Prayerful had simply believed the truth of God and repented of his sin, believing the gospel, and as a result, his sins were forgiven.

Beholding this scene again brought a flood of memories and thoughts to his mind. *Why would He do that for me? I was such a rotten man*, Prayerful's heart cried out. *What wonderful love this is!* A tear slipped out of Prayerful's eye as well and found its way down his cheek.

As he continued gazing at the scene, Prayerful could also discern the empty tomb at the base of the hill. This vacant grave filled his heart with joy, for he knew that three days after Christ had died, he arose, winning the greatest victory of history — a victory over sin and death. That same power, he knew, is available to all who believe.

As Prayerful stood up, blankly gazing at the

nearby trees, he was overcome with love and appreciation for what Christ had done on the cross, the memory of that sacrifice being renewed in his mind. He determined in his heart that he would do his utmost to faithfully love and serve such a wonderful Saviour.

After a minute, Half-Heart asked Prudent, "What else do you have for us to see?"

"Well, I only have one more place for you to look at," he answered.

In a few minutes, the telescope was once again adjusted, and Prayerful, who was still dwelling on the cross, was the first to look.

"I see a great hill," he explained after a short moment. Then, with excited recognition, he declared, "It is the Hill of Difficulty! I can see where the King's Road leads straight up that mountain.... Wait a minute.... I think I can see through the trees well enough to make out even more." After a slight pause, he continued, "I can see where the road splits. One way goes around the mountain."

"At Ease in Zion," Prudent confirmed.

"And the other road is Total Surrender. It heads up the steepest part of that hill."

Prayerful let the others have a turn while he recalled his trek up the Hill of Difficulty. "I remember that I was so excited after leaving the cross that I ascended that hill as quickly as possible. At the crossroads, I knew that God wanted me to take Total Surrender even though so many do not ... so without stopping, I went on up."

"That decision was certainly a wise one," Prudent affirmed. "It set you on the right road. But let me also give you a bit of warning. Although you already chose to take Total Surrender, you also must *daily* and even moment by moment choose to submit to

God's way. Pilgrims still have a tendency to try to do their own thing." Looking straight at Prayerful, he added, "Never forget the choice you made there, Prayerful." Prayerful nodded in understanding.

After a little more discussion about the sights they saw, everyone turned and began to descend the steps heading back down to ground level. Prayerful's mind was buzzing with thoughts. He blushed in shame, thinking how he had secretly longed for the comforts and pleasures of the world when his Saviour had given his all and died for him. Prayerful, filled with a renewal of passion, determined that he would press on with his journey for the Lord.

When they were about half-way down the steps of the tower, another thought occurred to him. *I also somewhat forgot why I am on this journey. It is a mission for the King ... to know Him and to deliver Passionate for Truth's sword to the one who is to bear it next.* His heart swelled with excitement, and shivers ran down his spine as he thought of the great task that was his.

In a short time, everyone was back on the first floor, and they knew that the time had come to move on. They packed their things and soon were ready to go. They all met outside the tower door, and the four friends looked a few yards away to The Road of Seeking. Prayerful saw that the name of the road changed here. It was now called The Path of Dedication.

As Prudent waived goodby, he gave one final admonition, "Remember the things you have seen here today; but also, remember, you cannot live in the past. You must keep pressing on and seeking higher ground. Near-to-God Mountain must always be your ultimate goal."

"Thank you!" they all called out. "Farewell!"

The Bridge

Twigs snapped beneath Prayerful's feet as he marched onward, up the forested hill. With each step, he thought of how these hills were quite a different landscape than the plains where their journey had begun. The beautiful farmland and grassy fields had faded away into forests, broken up by occasional lumber camps and homesteads. By now, the group had found that they were often climbing or descending some sort of hill, and they were quite thankful when the trail would either go through a ravine or along a level ridge.

When they reached the top of the hill which they had been climbing, Prayerful decided that everyone needed to take a short break; they had not had any time to rest since lunch and were a little tired out. Half-Heart plopped down on the trunk of a fallen tree and tried to catch his breath. Steadfast and Gentleness found a nearby rock to sit on while Prayerful pulled out his canteen and took several swallows of the lukewarm water.

"We should be sure to refill all of our canteens at the next stream," Steadfast stated.

"Alright," Prayerful confirmed as he put the lid back on his water container. "We can do that."

"I don't believe it will be too long before we find some either," Gentleness added. "I think I hear a waterfall in the distance."

They all sat still, silently listening, and were able to discern the rumble of a waterfall somewhere ahead. Prayerful began to wonder if this body of water would parallel their trail, or if they would have to cross it. They had already waded a number of streams thus far, but only one of them was large enough to be challenging. If they did have to cross it, this large stream — or river — could pose a challenge.

"How much longer till we reach some kind of civilization?" Half-Heart questioned, interrupting Prayerful's thoughts.

"That is very hard to say," Prayerful answered, turning to his companion. "We are not likely to find a city around here — the land is too hilly. However, I am sure that there are a few small towns and villages around. The real question is whether the road will lead through one of them. If so, we can certainly stop for supplies and even spend a night. But I doubt we will have such an opportunity any time soon."

"Yea, I guess that figures...." Half-Heart replied in a frustrated tone. "We have been traveling for several weeks now, trying to survive on wild nuts, berries, and fish ... or any other wild game that we can get. I know the homesteaders have been nice to let us stay in their barns at night, but I would just like to have an actual room somewhere. I know you guys are convinced that Take it Easy was some kind of bad guy, but I wish we could have stayed there at least a little longer."

"We are not opposed to finding nice places to stay and rest," Steadfast interjected, "but any place we go must be approved by the King. If He does not give us a beautiful palace to stay in, then so be it. We must be content ..."

"I just want a break from what we have been doing. Ok?!" Half-Heart angrily snapped.

"We understand," Prayerful gently replied. "The journey which the King has called us to is not always easy. There are certainly many parts we don't enjoy.... But we just need to make sure that wherever we go for rest has been placed there by God and not the enemy. I do not want to let my guard down again."

Half-Heart huffed but otherwise had no reply to this. Instead, he crossed his arms and scowled, staring off into the distance. After a few moments of awkward silence, Half-Heart stood up and grumbled, "Well, we should keep going." He then turned and began to plod down the trail, not waiting for everyone else. The others got up and followed after him, catching up quickly.

Even after walking for a few minutes, Prayerful was still a little stunned at Half-Heart's previous outburst. He had observed that ever since staying at the Palace of Christian Relaxation, Half-Heart's attitude had begun to change. At first, he merely lacked his former zeal, but as they progressed further down The Path of Dedication, he grew more irritable and testy. Consequently, Prayerful found that he always had to be careful around Half-Heart, for the slightest thing could set him off.

They continued along a ridge as the sound of the falls escalated, and before long, the noise grew loud enough that everyone knew they were very close. The trail led them down a short hill, and soon they descended into a beautiful, grassy clearing within a little valley. In the middle of this valley, lay a small river, creating a peaceful-looking landscape. About one hundred fifty yards to their left, the water plummeted over a picturesque waterfall overlooking another beautiful valley. Directly in front of them stood a bridge spanning the waterway.

Instinctively, the group strolled to the edge of the waterfall and peered over the cliff. They saw that after the water tumbled over the edge, it crashed into a rocky pool one hundred feet below. Prayerful's heart leapt into his throat, and he backed away once he saw the drop-off and the rocky scene at the base of the falls — he was afraid of heights.

Soon, everyone meandered back over to the bridge where they found a sign which read:

> *The King has decreed that in this Valley of*
> *Love, all Pilgrims must cross the Renouncing*
> *River at Cross Bearing Point. They must not*
> *traverse the Bridge of Selfish Choice.*

The seal of the Celestial City was imprinted in the bottom right hand corner of the sign, signifying its authenticity.

Prayerful glanced up and down the waterway till he noticed another marker thirty yards upstream from the bridge. *That must be Cross Bearing Point*, Prayerful figured. However, the thought of wading or swimming through this river brought fear to his heart as he realized how close they were to the falls.

Half-Heart was the first to voice his opinion. "This is crazy. We are supposed to swim across a river just a few yards away from a deadly waterfall. What kind of insanity is this?" After another moment, he added, "I think it's pretty obvious that we should cross over the bridge. Don't you agree?"

Even though he was terrified of the danger, Prayerful knew that his life was not his own. Mustering all of the courage he could find, he announced, "The Lord knows what he is doing…. There must be some reason for this. We need to go through Cross Bearing Point."

"What?!" responded Half-Heart. "Are you out of your mind? You have no idea what kind of undercurrent is out there!" he exclaimed, waving his hands in the air. "Even if you are a great swimmer, you will have a hard time fighting the current, and you could be swept over those falls before you know it!"

"I know," Prayerful replied as his courage strengthened. "But my life belongs to God, and this is what He wants me to do."

"Look," Half-Heart retorted, "this is the Valley of Love. How could a loving King send you through such deep waters?… I don't think He would do that. There must be some kind of mistake; that bridge is perfectly safe. Let me show you."

Half-Heart ran up to the bridge and walked several steps onto its floorboards. He then jumped up and down several times to demonstrate its strength. The bridge certainly did seem to be unshakeable.

Standing there, he shouted above the noise of the falls, "See, it is perfectly safe. What is wrong with crossing a little bridge?"

Prayerful's courage swelled within him as he spoke, "It doesn't matter how safe or practical it seems. It is still wrong to go against the King's decree. Besides," he continued, reaching down to the very bottom of his heart to finish, "I want to obey his command because … I love him." Without saying another word, Prayerful marched over to Cross Bearing Point and began preparing for his trek across the river.

Looking at Steadfast, Half-Heart pointed at Prayerful and exclaimed, "He's crazy!"

"No, he is right," Steadfast replied. "We need to go through the river." Without saying another word, he and Gentleness joined Prayerful. Half-Heart grumbled and remained in a foul mood, while the others tried to encourage him to go with them. Finally, he reluctantly agreed.

In order to keep their things dry, the pilgrims laid their shields on the ground and placed their swords and travel bags on them. They then strapped it all down, securing everything to the shields. Half-Heart had quite a bit of trouble with this, for his bag was so large and full that no matter what he did, things continually spilled out onto the ground. For the first time, Prayerful saw some of the other items that Half-Heart had packed. He was especially shocked when he saw several of the books: *My Plans*, *My Goals*, and *My Ideas*.

"You may have to leave some of those unneeded things behind," Steadfast stated when he saw the useless baggage.

Half-Heart snapped and pointed his finger right at Steadfast's face, "These things are mine, and I will take them if I want to! I am not going to sacrifice all that I own just because you have your *ideal* method of taking a journey for the King." Prayerful wanted to reply, but he knew that it would simply cause further argument and get nowhere; Half-Heart was set in his way and refused to listen to anyone.

As soon as everyone was ready, they lifted their shields above their heads and prepared to cross. Half-Heart struggled to lift his shield, and he almost dropped all of his belongings more than once before he got it above his head. Prayerful then led the way into the water, followed by Gentleness, Steadfast, and then Half-Heart.

When they were knee deep, Prayerful was

shocked to find that the riverbed was lined with flat stones as if it were designed to be a street. The more he thought on this, the more he became convinced that if they strayed off the path in the river, they would be stepping on the typical, uneven terrain and jagged rocks of a riverbed.

As they kept pressing on, step after step, they went deeper and deeper into the river. Soon, they were treading through water that was almost up to their shoulders, yet, amazingly, they had not noticed any current strong enough to sweep them away. Every step, though, was difficult as they pushed their way through the water. Prayerful was thankful that, through it all, their footing remained sure.

Within a matter of minutes, the group began the gradual ascent toward the other side of the river. They kept up their steady pace and were soon on the riverbank. Only when his feet were on dry ground again did Prayerful let his shield down and breathe a sigh of relief. When he turned around, however, his heart sank. Although Steadfast and Gentleness stood only a few feet away, Half-Heart was not with them.

Prayerful scanned the waterway and saw no sign of his friend. "Where is Half-Heart?" he asked frantically, hoping that he had not lost his footing and been swept away.

After a few moments, Gentleness pointed, "He is over there on the other side of the river."

Apparently, while they were crossing, Half-Heart had turned around and returned back to shore. By now, he had his bag on his shoulder again and his shield resting on his back. He, evidently, had given up on the idea of crossing through the river and was heading toward the bridge. Prayerful shook his head in disappointment.

Soon, the clomp, clomp of Half-Heart's boots could be heard pounding on the wooden planks and reverberating above the noise of the falls. Looking at Half-Heart's expression, Prayerful thought that his friend seemed almost proud of the decision he had made. Steadfast, Gentleness, and Prayerful walked over to where the bridge ended on their side of the river and were ready to meet Half-Heart, but no one was prepared for what happened next.

When Half-Heart was two-thirds of the way across, Prayerful turned toward Steadfast and Gentleness to discuss how much farther they should travel before setting up camp. The moment he opened his mouth, everyone heard a loud *crack* followed by Half-Heart's scream. They turned just in time to see his head and arms disappear through the broken flooring of the bridge.

The following splash was met with a blur of activity on shore. Prayerful and Steadfast sprinted downstream, around the bridge, and came to the water's edge. In the river, Half-Heart flailed his arms, desperately trying to fight the current, but here it was quite strong. Steadfast cast his belongings aside and dove into the water. With strength and endurance, he fought his way toward a panicking Half-Heart who was trying to battle the current. Within a minute, Steadfast was able to grab Half-Heart and pull him onto a rock that projected out of the torrent.

Despite the safety of the boulder, they were still in danger. They could not swim to the riverbank because the current was far too strong here and they were right next to the falls. Prayerful stood on the bank at a loss, not knowing what to do. At that moment, Gentleness appeared next to him with Steadfast's rope.

"Do you think you can reach them with this?"

she questioned.

"I think so," he answered, taking it from her. He took several coils in his right hand and held onto the other end of the rope with his left. Just as he was about to throw it, he spotted Half-Heart's bag plunge over the waterfall. This sight made him fear even more for the safety of his friends as his mind quickly pictured one of them facing such a fate.

Using all of his strength, Prayerful launched the rope as far out as possible. It landed several yards above the rock, and the current quickly carried it downriver to where Steadfast and Half-Heart were waiting. Both of the men took the rope and tied it around themselves, preparing to jump into the water again. Fear threatened to envelop Prayerful, for he knew that one wrong move could send his comrades over the edge. He hoped that he and Gentleness had enough strength to pull them in against the current. "Make haste to help me, O Lord of my salvation," Prayerful silently prayed as he prepared himself for the task of hauling them to shore.

At Prayerful's signal, the two men jumped into the water, and Prayerful and Gentleness began to tug on the rope with all of their strength. Since they were a little upriver from Steadfast and Half-Heart, Prayerful and Gentleness were fighting against the current while trying to draw them to shore. Working together, however, they were able to bring in inch after inch of rope. The two men in the swift water could not do much to help, and everyone was afraid that Prayerful and Gentleness' strength would give out.

The minutes passed, and slowly more and more of the rope lay on the shore as the men were drawn closer and closer. Before too long, Steadfast and Half-Heart stumbled out of the water. As soon as the men were freed from the rope, everyone collapsed in the soft grass, exhausted.   Although Half-Heart's belongings and shield had been lost, relief flooded over everyone now that he had been rescued.

They lay there silently for a while, worn out from the strain of the rescue.   While resting, Prayerful realized that if a person tried to save everything he could for this life, he will lose it all; but those who are willing to give it all up for the Lord will have great gain.

Clashing Steel

Prayerful's eyes slowly opened as the dawning sun glimmered through the trees. The soft roar of the falls in the distant background was a continual reminder of the dangers they had faced yesterday, and Prayerful instantly remembered the events of Half-Heart's rescue. After the incident at the waterfall, they had considered camping out near the river, but everyone thought it best to make a little more progress before nightfall. Although they spent the night further down the trail, the sound of the falls still had hushed them to sleep.

Sitting up, he stretched his arms out and glanced over to where Steadfast had built a fire last night. It was out, but Prayerful was sure there would be a few coals remaining. Standing up, he meandered over to where they had piled some small branches and collected some kindling to build the fire again. Thankfully, the dry leaves and small sticks quickly started to burn, and soon he was sitting next to the crackling flames, waiting for the others to stir.

Prayerful continued to think on Half-Heart's close call yesterday and was filled with pity for his friend. He wished that Half-Heart had listened to everyone else, left the unneeded things behind, and waded through the river. However, what bothered Prayerful the most was that Half-Heart did not merely lose his shield; Prayerful saw him deliberately throw it into the river after Steadfast had pulled him to the rock. Prayerful bowed his head for a few minutes, interceding for his friend.

Soon, everyone was up, going through their morning routine. After finishing their breakfast of bread, butter, and ham, which was given to them by the last homesteader they stayed with, they put out the fire and packed their things. They were all hoping for a quiet, uneventful day but had no idea what danger lay several hours down the trail.

After leaving camp, Prayerful led the group along the trail, enjoying the sights and smells of the forest. They traveled over hills and through valleys, crossing an occasional stream. As the day wore on, Prayerful observed that the sky became more and more overcast, and the air gradually grew more moist. *I hope if we get any rain that it will at least wait till after dark.*

After taking a brief stop for their noon meal, they approached a beautiful grassy valley surrounded on all sides by lush, wooded hills. When they came to the edge of the meadow, they observed a large sign noting the name of this vale: The Battlefield of the Heart. When Prayerful saw the words of the sign, he instinctively glanced up to analyze the field before him. A quick look told him that it was, indeed, the ideal place for a conflict between two armies, for the level battlefield was interrupted by only a few boulders and an occasional cluster of trees.

As they continued studying the scene before them, everyone noticed that there were four castles on the hills surrounding this valley. They eventually learned that these fortresses were known as The Castles of Earthly Attachment. The one farthest away from them on the left was, by far, the largest. While beholding these structures, apprehension began to swell in Prayerful's heart as he sensed danger ahead.

On the far end of the field, the hills from either side of the vale rose up and joined together to form great cliffs broken up by one narrow pass. After crossing the battlefield, The Path of Dedication led through that narrow pass which appeared to be the only way out of this place. There was no avoiding this battlefield.

As they stepped out into the grassland, Prayerful's senses were on full alert. He had no idea if they would run into danger or not, so he kept a constant lookout for any sign of trouble. Taking extra caution, he removed his shield from his back, preparing for a surprise attack.

They proceeded cautiously for a while without seeing anything. Once they were close to a third of the way through the field, Prayerful began to wonder if they might get through this place without trouble at all since they had not yet seen any sign of danger.

Within a minute, his hopes were dashed, for out from behind the nearest cluster of trees strolled four men heading their direction. Prayerful was a little confused, however, for the strangers were dressed in the fanciest of clothing, decked with gold and silver. They each had a long cloak, and Prayerful could not see any sign of weaponry. From their appearances, they seemed harmless, but Prayerful refused to relax his guard.

Once these large men were within fifteen feet, they stopped and opened their arms in reception. "Welcome to our valley," the man who appeared to be the leader warmly declared. "What brings you here?"

Still desiring to be cautious, Prayerful answered,

"We are merely Pilgrims on a journey."

"We tend to have many Pilgrims come through here.... Many of them are destined for Near-to-God Mountain. Can I assume that is where you are headed?" Without waiting for an answer, he introduced himself, "I am Mr. Covetous. These are my good friends, Pride, Personal Ambition, and Love of Pleasure. We own the castles that you see on the hilltops around here."

"We couldn't help but notice how impressive they looked," Half-Heart stated.

"If you think they are nice on the outside, you should see the inside," Pride replied. "Anyone who enters will feel like nobility."

"And more than that," Love of Pleasure continued, "there are fun surprises around every corner, and ..." he paused to let his words take effect, "there seems to be no end to what a person can do for enjoyment. If you don't believe us, just ask anyone who has ever visited, and they will tell you how wonderful it is."

Appearing to change the topic, Personal Ambition questioned, "Have you been camping out a lot on your journey?"

"Yes, we have," Half-Heart answered with a tone of frustration.

"That's what I figured," Covetous interjected. "I can imagine that must be quite difficult. You *do* look worn out.... You know, I was just thinking, it looks like we might get some rain here soon," he stated, glancing up at the sky. "Why don't you good Pilgrims be my guest tonight? I will give you anything you want.... You deserve it with the long journey you have been on."

Prayerful's heart initially leapt at the offer, for he would certainly love to take a break from the journey and enjoy himself. However, he knew that the treasures of these men would only be consumed upon his lust, and that this was not something that God wanted for them. It was only his flesh that sought such pleasures. Despite this knowledge, the decision was not as easy as he had imagined, for the temptation to join these men was strong. Prayerful thought of the treasures of the castles, and then he reflected on the greatest treasures of all: those in the Celestial City. He wrestled between the desires of his flesh and the will of God. Eventually, knowing that his heart would be where his treasure was, he determined to do what was right.

"Thank you," he said, refusing their offer, "but we really must be going."

"But I insist!" Covetous said in a sincere sounding tone. "I will even host a banquet for you with all sorts of food and give you a grand tour of my castle."

"That sounds wonderful!" Half-Heart exclaimed.

"Half-Heart, we need to keep going," Steadfast urged. "Don't forget our journey."

Prayerful rejoiced inwardly that Steadfast recognized the danger and was trying to prevent Half-Heart from making another bad choice.

"There is no harm in taking a break from our journey for the King," Half-Heart retorted as he rolled his eyes at Steadfast. "Unless you think I am being foolish, don't forget *I* volunteered to take this trip unlike so many others.... And if I remember right, no one on this journey has spoken more of the King than me. So you can't accuse me of not being spiritually minded!"

"Sounds to me like I will have at least one guest at my table tonight," Covetous announced as he stretched out his hand to Half-Heart.

"Don't let the love of the world pull you away," Prayerful said to Half-Heart, but his efforts were in vain. Before he knew it, Half-Heart walked over to Covetous and shook his hand. "Half-Heart, wait …" he began to say.

"Stop being so uptight," Half-Heart shot back. "You will be the ones missing out on a good time. You guys are too strict.… It would do you some good to lighten up a little and enjoy what this world has to offer."

"When you are ready, my doors will be open to the rest of you as well," Covetous said as he turned to lead Half-Heart away.

Prayerful and the others watched in shock as their close friend was escorted across the field toward the largest castle. Prayerful knew this was a bad mistake and was determined that he would not fall for this trap as well. Seeing Half-Heart and Covetous disappear behind a cluster of trees, he felt for the handle of his sword and was prepared to run.

"I can understand your reservation," Love of Pleasure stated. "I am sure that you have had to face multiple enemies on your journey. That must have been hard for you, and I am sure that you don't want to face any more. But I have to imagine that you must be tired of your journey. Surely, you would like to have some time where you can enjoy yourself."

Prayerful stood there silently, not giving heed to the words Love of Pleasure spoke — his heart was fixed. Steadfast, Gentleness, and Prayerful were set on seeking those things which are above.

"The King *does* ordain rest for us and gives us things to enjoy, but it does not come through the love of the world," Steadfast retorted.

"Don't worry," Love of Pleasure continued, "we won't force you to come with us." He gave a slight pause, and then added in a darker voice, "Because when we are done with you, you will *want* to come!"

In a flash, these three man shed their gorgeous robes, and with a swish, they each pulled out a sword that had been hidden under their clothing. Only now did Prayerful fully recognize what these large men truly were: giants of evil.

Without hesitation, three more swords were yanked from their scabbards. Prayerful and his friends stood their ground with courage, knowing that they had to be wary of the blades of their enemies whose sharp edges had been poisoned with Lust. The Battlefield of the Heart was about to see another fight.

Love of Pleasure attacked Prayerful with vengeance, and the noise of clanging steel echoed through the valley. Though it was not his first time facing an enemy, it was difficult for Prayerful to quell his trembling heart. He tried to follow what he had learned in previous battles and not let fear or pride be his downfall. He needed to rely upon the power of the King's sword and not his own ability.

Swords clashed time and time again as the three friends stood their ground, unwilling to let the enemy penetrate their defenses. Prayerful then decided to go on the attack and began bringing blow after blow upon his enemy, forcing him to retreat. Then, in the middle of the fight, he cried out, "Lay not up for yourselves treasures upon earth." Love of Pleasure seemed to cringe at this, and Prayerful took advantage of his opponent's hesitation. He attacked with speed and the power of the Sword of the Spirit. Soon, Love of Pleasure, cradling a wounded arm, was retreating toward the nearest castle on the northern side of the valley.

Prayerful turned just in time to see the other two giants disengage as well. These enemies retreated in the same direction as their comrade. Prayerful was glad the fight was over. He did think it odd, though, that these giants did not battle any longer then they did.

"We need to move fast," Steadfast declared as everyone tried to catch their breath. "I know how these giants in this Battlefield of the Heart operate.... They will be back soon.... Their plan is to attack, retreat, and attack again.... They will keep doing this to wear us down and try to catch us off our guard." Taking another deep breath, he added, "As we go, keep a constant look out.... They will come after us when we don't expect it."

The trio took off at a moderate run toward the pass, hoping to get there soon. Passing by a large pile of rocks, everyone kept vigilant, but their enemies did not appear. As they hasted, they scanned the region and could not see any sign of trouble. Right when it seemed like the giants would leave them be, their three enemies leapt out from behind some nearby trees and charged the faithful group of pilgrims.

Personal Ambition took on Prayerful this time, and he had to adjust his fight with this new giant. Once again, he sought to rely upon the power of the King's sword and found that it did not fail him. He was able to quickly put this opponent on the retreat, and it did not take long before all three of their enemies were once again running off out of sight. Prayerful and his friends only took a few moments of heavy breathing before they picked up their quick pace again.

As they ran along, they continued to keep constant watch on every tree and rock but saw no sign of their adversaries. The further they ran, the greater Prayerful's apprehension grew, for he figured that these evil giants had some kind of devious plan. He sensed that the fight was not yet over.

As they neared the pass, hope began to rise in his heart, for it appeared that the giants would not be able to squeeze through the ravine — it was too narrow for them. *If we can only get there before the giants appear!* At this thought, he picked up the pace.

Just as they were a few yards away, their foes appeared out of nowhere. In a flash, Prayerful had his shield up and was prepared for the fight. However, he noticed that they were in greater danger than before, for this time Covetous joined his three wicked companions in their deed of evil. The odds did not look good: four against three.

Love of Pleasure and Personal Ambition immediately brought their swords to bear against Steadfast and Gentleness while Prayerful faced Covetous and Pride alone. He had never faced two enemies at once and was terrified, knowing that his attention would have to be divided between two poisoned swords of evil. Instead of immediately attacking, however, these giants waited in silence for a few moments.

"What is so bad with the things we are offering you?" Covetous questioned with a hurt look on his face.

"All that is in the world, the lust of the flesh, the lust of the eyes, and the pride of life, is not of the Father, but is of the world," Prayerful replied defiantly.

"Come on, it can't be that bad," Pride replied. "Just think how these things will make you look to everyone else."

For a small moment, Prayerful began to reconsider what they were saying. *Certainly it would be nice to be respected,* he thought. In his moment of consideration, he dropped his shield a few inches for a brief second. Covetous took advantage of this mild hesitation and swiped at Prayerful's sword arm, catching him off guard.

Time seemed to slow as he saw Covetous' sword

race toward his shoulder; however, out of the corner of his eye, Prayerful saw Steadfast lunging at Covetous. Steadfast shouted, "Yield not to temptation!" What Prayerful saw in the next several seconds left him stunned. Steadfast masterfully blocked Covetous' weapon with his own sword, and then, using the momentum from his lunge, he crashed into the giant, causing both of them to tumble to the ground. Prayerful did not have time to watch his friend unload all of his skill on the giant, for he had his own fight to deal with.

Prayerful quickly brought several blows upon Pride and sent him into an immediate retreat. At that instant, Prayerful heard something behind him, and he spun around with his shield in position just in time to block an attack from Personal Ambition. Knowing that he was once again facing two enemies, he adjusted his position so that they were both in front of him — he did not want the giants to surround him, diverting his attention more than necessary. This time, he did not allow them the chance to speak but attacked them both with fury and the power of the Sword of the Word.

Prayerful knew that these enemies of all righteousness would continue their relentless attack, so he quickly developed a plan. Shouting toward his friends, he said, "Set your affection on things above, not on things on the earth. We need to get through the Pass of Eternal Focus."

While swords were clashing and everyone was deep in his own fight, Prayerful, Steadfast, and Gentleness were able to maneuver themselves so that they were soon fighting side by side and the giants were all in front of them. Gradually, they moved their way over to the pass, working as a team defending and helping each other.

When they got in the right position, Gentleness

was the first to squeeze through the rocky gap to safety. The two men continued fighting until Prayerful found a quick break in the battle, and then he, too, lunged though the opening. He then turned to watch what would happen to Steadfast.

With one final yell and sweep of his sword, Steadfast caused all of his foes to jump back away from its razor sharp tip. Then, he quickly backed through the opening, keeping the point of his sword aimed toward the four giants. These enemies stood at the entrance of the pass and watched as the three Pilgrims retreated to safety. As they backed further and further into the gorge, Prayerful could hear the giants in a heated argument, blaming each other over their failure to capture the Pilgrims.

Once they were beyond the sight of their enemies, Prayerful, Steadfast, and Gentleness turned their full attention to what was in front of them as they slowly made their way through the pass in single file. The path remained quite narrow for a long time, so they could not stop for a break, but after an hour, they finally exited the narrow gorge and stepped out into a beautiful, green field. The moist breeze and dark clouds signaled that rain certainly was imminent.

Gentleness pointed to their right toward the edge of the woods. "Can we camp out there tonight?"

"I think that would be a perfect spot," Steadfast replied.

Though they felt a little sore from the fight earlier, they moved swiftly to the location selected by Gentleness, dropped their bags, and began to set up camp. Gentleness collected wood and started a fire while the men worked as quickly as possible to build a waterproof shelter. A low rumble echoed across the land as Gentleness watched the first tiny flames eat away at the leaves and kindling.

After fifteen minutes, Steadfast and Prayerful were finished with their lean-to and were satisfied with their work. They then set all the dry wood they could find into their shelter. Before long, the rain began to fall in torrents, and the three of them finally sat down to rest, the shelter keeping them perfectly dry.

After a few minutes of silently watching the storm, Prayerful turned to Steadfast and said, "Thank you for saving me back there."

"You're welcome, my friend. I know you would have done the same for me."

"I am sorry I let my guard down," Prayerful stated as he hung his head.

"I understand. I have done the same before," Steadfast replied. "But that is why God gave us friends: two are better than one. And don't forget, a man sharpeneth the countenance of his friend." He paused for a second, and then added, "I have found a certain thing always helps me whenever I am tempted to let earthly affections pull on my heart.... Actually, I used it today."

"What is it?" Prayerful questioned.

"When Personal Ambition came after me, he, too, spoke before he fought. Instead of listening, I raised my sword in front of my face so that my eyes could see the handle. On the hilt of our swords is engraved a cross and a crown. These things always remind me what is truly important: to love my King who died for me. Just a little look at the hilt brings things back into perspective."

"Thank you," Prayerful said as he thought about the advice. "Both of you are truly great friends.

To the Rescue

"We have to do something to help Half-Heart!" Gentleness exclaimed with urgency. The thought of their friend possibly bound in shackles immediately flashed through Prayerful's mind as he realized the situation Half-Heart might be in.

"I really don't know if he would listen to us," Steadfast replied. "After all, the backslider is filled with *his own* ways."

"But he is our brother in Christ," Gentleness rebutted, her eyes filled with determination. "Maybe by now he sees how wrong his choice was and wants to escape."

"It is too risky," Steadfast stated. "It is more likely that he is completely blind to the fact that he is in captivity, and we would be putting ourselves in great danger for nothing."

With passionate persistence, she continued, "We can't just leave him behind — especially if he is a prisoner! We have to do something!"

Steadfast did not reply, but turned his head and looked out into the darkness of the rainy night. Prayerful watched as Steadfast wrestled with Gentleness' plea. Prayerful certainly understood

Steadfast's reservation; after all, who would want to sneak into a giant's abode and try to rescue someone who probably doesn't even want to leave? Yet, he also understood Gentleness' perspective, for Half-Heart was a fellow Pilgrim … and a friend.

"I think we should at least try," Prayerful said after a slight pause. "At the very least, we must do our part to help him … even if he refuses to leave."

Steadfast continued staring into the darkness without saying a word.   As Prayerful examined Steadfast's expressionless face, he could not determine what the man was thinking, but he knew that a silent struggle was raging inside this faithful warrior.

After a few moments of quiet pondering, Steadfast replied, "All right, we will go. Let's hope for the best."

*   *   *

After the sun arose on that cloudy morning and they finished their daily routine, the trio spent most of the morning hours making their way across the hilltops, hoping to come at the fortress from an unexpected angle. They had already discussed some plans for the rescue throughout the previous evening but knew that they would have to wait to see the situation in order to finalize their ideas.

When they were within sight of Covetous' castle, Love of Treasure, they looked for the highest hill nearby in order to reconnoiter the situation. Before long, they found the perfect spot and soon settled down in a secluded area to examine the fortress.

From this vantage point, they could make out that there was a massive outer wall which surrounded the great keep. From what they could see, there was very little activity inside the castle walls, and things seemed to be quiet.

After several hours of observation, they were mystified by the fact that there seemed to be no extra guards. The giant appeared to be the only enemy present, keeping watch over an unknown number of prisoners. While pondering the situation, they were also saddened by the fact that, apparently, none of the hostages tried to escape, even when the giant was gone. The trio guessed that these prisoners might be fed with the Food of Addiction causing them to want to remain with the giant.

Around noon, they left their lookout spot and retreated to a nearby cluster of rocks where they were able to discuss their strategy. All afternoon, the three of them labored to come up with a definite plan but to no avail. After a while of consideration, they decided that the best idea was to somehow sneak into the castle at night when everyone was asleep. The problem was that the fortress seemed impregnable, and the doors and gates appeared to be locked all the time. They were stuck.

Later in the afternoon, Steadfast snuck back to the lookout position to see if he could find anything they had missed. He was up there for about half an hour before he returned, and when he arrived, Prayerful could see that he was quite eager to speak.

"I am pretty sure I saw Half-Heart inside the walls," he explained. "He was in chains but didn't seem to care. All around him were all sorts of things … lusts of the world. Some of them were within arm's length; others, were farther away. He seemed to be constantly reaching for the things that were beyond his grasp, always trying to get more. He honestly looked quite pitiful." Hearing these words, Prayerful grew even more determined to rescue him.

After a minute, Prayerful asked, "Did you have any more ideas come to you?"

"Yes. Right before I saw Half-Heart, I noticed a tree branch reaching over the wall on the far side of the castle, and it looked strong enough to hold a man's weight. If we could climb up the tree and out onto the branch, we could lower the Rope of Spiritual Fervor over the inside of the wall. Then, if there is a problem, we could use the rope to get back out."

"That might work," thought Prayerful, "as long as we don't wake the giant and have to get out in a hurry."

"There is another problem.… We don't know where to find Half-Heart in the castle," Steadfast continued.

They thought on this next dilemma throughout the rest of the day and continually prayed for help. By evening, they still did not have any definite idea where to locate their friend. They figured they would at least look around and peer through windows to see what they could find. Though it may be futile, they would at least give it a try.

Before leaving for the castle, they also worked through various scenarios and plans on what to do if they were found out. They concluded that if they were discovered, they would first try to climb the rope and flee the castle. Their base camp among the rocks would be their rendezvous point in case they got separated. If they could not get over the wall soon enough, they may have to hide or even fight. No matter what, it would be risky.

As the land grew dim at twilight, they snuck closer to the castle but remained in the woods to conceal their movements. Thankfully, by now the clouds had vanished so that the moon would give them enough light. They slowly worked their way around to where the tree was located and soon found a place to hide. Once they were concealed behind some brush, the three pilgrims remained still, silently waiting for a late hour when everyone would be deep in sleep.

They waited for an agonizingly long hour, wishing to immediately go in and at the same time dreading the danger. All of a sudden, they heard a faint noise in the woods. Everyone froze as they listened closely, and soon they could distinguish a soft, methodic crumple of leaves and twigs.... Someone was moving through the woods behind them. The footsteps were faint at first, but the sound steadily grew in volume. Fear began to well up in Prayerful's heart as his imagination began to run wild. Everyone remained motionless, watching and waiting to see what would happen. They did not have to wait long, for after only a few seconds a man appeared between the trees.

Prayerful could see enough to tell that this stranger was not one of the giants; this realization brought him a little relief from his fears. In the dim light of the half moon and starlit sky, they could make out that this man exuded strength and confidence. Since he was walking about so boldly in this region of evil, Prayerful had to assume the worst about him. He could not fathom who this man was, and thus remained motionless, afraid of being found out.

The stranger continued on his way straight toward the castle — and their hiding place. When he was within several yards of where the pilgrims were concealed, the man stopped and gazed at their hiding spot. The trio held their breath, their hearts pounding.

"Good Pilgrims," the man spoke softly, "I am Help. For many, many years now I have been serving the King by giving assistance to Pilgrims in need. I am here to unlock the gate for you. Your friend is in the dungeon.... You will find that he still has his torch burning. Look for a window two feet off the ground on the north side of the castle. You will be able to see the light from his torch. Do what you can to show him his sin, but remember that he must make his own decision." Without another word, he turned toward the castle and walked right up to the rear gate.

Prayerful watched as Help pulled something from his pocket and reached for the latch. The distinct click of a lock being opened reached Prayerful's ears, and he looked on as Help effortlessly pushed open the massive door, silently swinging it inward. Prayerful was relieved that the hinges did not squeak.

After Help disappeared back through the woods, the three friends left the safety of their hiding place and silently crept toward the open door. Prayerful's heart raced and his hands shook as they passed through the doorway into the abode of evil. When they were inside the castle grounds, they could see that everything was dark and still. The inner grounds of the castle were vast, for the keep lay over eight hundred feet away from the outer wall. Just as they had observed previously, this area was littered with more items of lust than Prayerful knew existed.

The trio slowly circled the grounds, keeping an eye out for the light that Help told them about. Passing by many darkened windows, Prayerful wondered how many prisoners were trapped by this monster of evil. Soon, they came to a small window with a flickering glow coming from inside. *This must be it*, Prayerful thought.

They tiptoed up to the window and peered in. Prayerful was not prepared for what he saw inside, and it took him a minute to recover from the shock. Half-Heart was sitting at a table loaded with all sorts of food. He was eating, seemingly oblivious to the fact that his hands and feet were bound by the shackles of sin. His tunic of the King was stained with dirt and mud. Though he was enjoying a sumptuous meal, Half-Heart looked quite miserable.

Glancing about the room, Prayerful saw that the wealth of the castle seemed to fill the space. This was one of the cells known as Idols of the Heart. Prayerful's heart sank even further when he spotted Half-Heart's sword cast aside into the farthest corner.

"Half-Heart," Prayerful spoke softly, "Half-Heart!"

Half-Heart snapped his head up and around, gazing toward the window and searching for the voice calling him. At this, Prayerful stuck his head far enough into the room to let the light of the torch illuminate his face.

"What are you doing here?" Half-Heart asked, obviously surprised.

"We have come to get you out of here."

"Why?" Half-Heart questioned.

"You are a prisoner!" Prayerful was a little dumbfounded at his friend's confusion.

After a slight pause, Half-Heart replied, "What are you talking about?" With a bewildered expression, he continued, "I am not a prisoner.... I am an honored guest."

"But you have chains around your hands and feet!"

Half-Heart furrowed his brow and responded, "I don't have any chains on me. I am as free as I ever have been. It is wonderful here! You would love it!"

"Your hands and feet are in shackles," Prayerful

tried again.

Half-Heart lifted up his right arm, glanced at his wrists, and then said, "I don't see anything. What kind of joke is this?"

"I can see the chains as plain as anything. You are a prisoner here. Covetous has no intention of ever letting you go free…. We came to help you get out of here. I am sure that if you confess your sin of idolatry, those shackles will fall off your hands."

"I am having the time of my life here, and I have no idea what you are talking about. I am *not* a prisoner, and I am *not* in bonds," Half-Heart repeated.

Exasperated, Prayerful tried a different approach. "I can tell your heart is set on the things that the world loves…. You shouldn't let your heart envy sinners. The Lord has commanded that we are *not* to love the world or even the things in the world. This castle isn't where the Lord wants you."

"I think you are just going to an extreme," Half-Heart said as he took another bite of the Fruit of Callousness.

"Don't eat that!" Prayerful exclaimed. "If you harden your heart, you will fall into more mischief!"

"My heart is just fine. I have done more for God than many other Pilgrims out there. I am just taking some time to enjoy myself for a while…. I will be just fine."

"But," retorted Prayerful, growing desperate, "those who trust in their own hearts are fools. Besides, what about our pilgrimage?"

"When I am done here, I will go on," Half-Heart stated with an air of indifference as he turned back to his meal.

Prayerful did not know what more he could say. After a few moments, one more thought came to him.

"Don't forget, Half-Heart, we are to love God with all our heart, soul, mind, and strength."

"I do love God!" Half-Heart shot back with a piercing glare.

"If you really love Him, wouldn't you want to get to Near-to-God Mountain?"

Half-Heart scowled at Prayerful, and then said, "I will get there someday. Now, leave me alone, and stop preaching at me!" Half-Heart pounded his fist into the table to make his point, staring up at Prayerful with fury in his eyes.

Prayerful backed away at this outburst. At that moment, he knew there was nothing more he could say to convince his friend of the truth. Half-Heart's love for the things of the world blinded him to reality, and he was willingly giving himself over to the bondage of sin.

Turning to Steadfast and Gentleness, Prayerful could see that they were shocked at his reaction as well. They were prepared for Half-Heart to refuse their help, but they were not ready for such an outburst. There was nothing more they could do to help their friend, and they all knew it.

"All right," Prayerful said to Half-Heart. "I guess we will be on our way."

Half-Heart just grunted and took another bite of the food in front of him. Prayerful got up, and with heavy hearts, the three of them retreated back toward the way they came. As they silently passed through the Gate of Choice, Prayerful thought, *If he would have only listened, he could be leaving this horrible place right now!*

Rockslide

Several days passed, and Prayerful could not get Half-Heart out of his mind. He could not believe that his friend and fellow companion had sacrificed knowing God for the treasures of this world. He was not the only one grieving, however, for everyone's previous joy seemed to have disappeared.

They stopped in a small village one evening so that they could resupply their food. Since it was so close to dusk, they spent the night among the hospitable townspeople and were able to tell them of Christ. The people of the village listened to them, but no one responded; at least the townsfolk remained quite friendly. Although the trio really enjoyed sleeping in real beds and having fresh cooked bread, they knew that they must press on. Thus early the next morning, they continued on down the trail.

The Path of Dedication led them onward, further and further into the hills. By now, they had grown accustomed to the constant shift in terrain, and they learned to appreciate the beauty of the mountains, rather than just looking at the challenges of the topography. Their journey, though difficult, allowed them to get into a routine again as they pressed onward toward their goal.

One day, while hiking along a ridge, the trail suddenly shifted to the left, leading them through the middle of a hillside. To their right, the steep elevation ascended up into the trees out of sight, and to their left, it sloped downward beyond their view as well. Now, not even their path was on level ground. This made progress even more difficult as it was easy to lose their footing.

Walking along the slope, they soon came to a break in the trees. As soon as they saw what was ahead, they instantly knew that this was a very dangerous section of the pathway.   Here, the steep slope was layered with stones and rocks precariously resting on the hillside. The smallest ones were just pebbles while some of the larger stones were the size of a giant cooking pot; however, there were a few even bigger than that. Evidently, no plant life could grow here, for many landslides seemed to have eroded away the entire slope. This was the Hill of Testing, and there was no way around it.

They did not have to be warned about the ever-present danger of a rockslide; thus, they each carefully watched their footing as they stepped out onto the rugged landscape.   While Prayerful led the group through the rough terrain, he took note of various stone outcroppings that stood ten feet above the rocky slope. These great boulders appeared to still be attached to the main mountain and were thus unmovable.

Thankfully, despite numerous rockslides, the path was still pretty clear through this place, for these gigantic boulders had been marked to point out where the path lay. Having to occasionally glance up to make sure that they were still on the right trail, everyone tried to keep their eyes on the ground in order to watch where their next step would land. Prayerful could see trees in the distance, and he calculated that they would have to trek this dangerous spot for about half a mile.

When they were about half-way through, they all paused at the sound of a low rumble coming from above them. Their eyes snapped around to their right, looking up the hill. Instantly, they saw a cloud of dust descending upon them as the noise grew louder. *Rockslide!* Prayerful instantly realized.

Panic swept over him as he tried to figure out what to do. They could not make it to the other side in time, nor could they go back; they only had moments to get to safety. Seeing the large ten-foot rock pillars, Prayerful had an idea.

"Get behind one of those boulders!" he shouted.

The nearest one was thirty feet behind them and they instantly bolted for it. They soon found that the uneven rocks at their feet made it impossible to go at a full run, but, thankfully, they were still able to move quickly.

When they were fifteen feet away from safety, Prayerful glanced up toward the dust cloud. His heart raced even faster when he saw individual rocks bouncing down toward them. Prayerful followed behind Gentleness and Steadfast as quickly as he could but wondered if it would be too late. He set his eyes on their goal, praying as he picked his way though the stony hillside.

As Gentleness drew near the large boulder, Prayerful glanced up at his two companions and saw a rock the size of a small dog bounce between Steadfast and Gentleness. Around the same time, he began seeing more and more smaller rocks flying all around him. His heart beat even faster, and he wondered if he would be carried on down to the bottom of the mountain, buried under tons of rocks.

Prayerful saw Gentleness jump behind the safety of the great pillar, and Steadfast was close behind. Right then, something struck Prayerful's left leg just below the knee. The blow was great enough that he was instantly thrown to the ground, and he began to slide down the hill along with the rocks and boulders that were bound for the valley below. As he slid downward, he grabbed at anything that might stop him, but all he could find were loose stones. Within moments, however, his hand grasped onto an immovable rock that kept him from going any further. Fear gripped his heart as he realized that he could still be smashed at any moment.

Several stones bounced off Prayerful's helmet and shield while he was continually sprayed with smaller pebbles. If he stayed there, he would, no doubt, be crushed and buried by the rocks. As quickly as he could, he got up to race to safety, but he collapsed because of a sharp pain in his leg. Not wanting to be buried alive, he began crawling toward the boulder, hoping that he did not have any broken bones. Rocks and stones continued to whiz past him, and some of them even grazed his helmet and shield. His arms quickly became bruised from the many stones pelting him, and he fell to the ground as some of the rocks beneath him also gave way.

Before he had made it three feet, he suddenly felt Steadfast's arm around his own. He glanced up, surprised that his friend had left the shelter of the great boulder. Steadfast helped him stand up as several more medium-sized rocks flew by, missing them by inches. They hobbled along, being constantly struck by stones and pebbles and were almost to safety when a stone whacked Prayerful in his right hand and he screamed. The pain made him want to stop, but Steadfast hauled him behind the Boulder of the Promises of God. Though it felt agonizingly long, his rescue had only taken a few seconds.

The three of them huddled behind their shelter as they continued to cough from the dust. Within moments, a wall of stones came crashing down the mountain as the main part of the rockslide came upon them. They remained there behind the safety of the rock for several minutes, waiting for the danger to pass.

When the last of the rocks tumbled to the valley below and the roar of the landslide diminished, everyone looked at one another in relief. It was only then that Prayerful noticed the throbbing pain in his hand and leg. His right hand was bleeding profusely from a large gash which would need to be treated immediately; however, Prayerful quickly realized that his leg was his worst injury. Pain shot through him whenever he tried to move it, and he was afraid it was broken.

Prayerful glanced up from looking at his own cuts and saw that Steadfast had also suffered several wounds. Gentleness, evidently, had made it to safety in time and had only one small cut on her arm. The Rocks of Hardship had certainly left their toll on the trio.

Gentleness immediately opened her bag, pulled out scraps of cloth, and began washing everyone's wounds, trying to prevent infection. Soon, all of the injuries were bound, but there was not much she could do about Prayerful's leg at the moment.

After everyone was bandaged, Steadfast helped Prayerful to his feet, supporting him as they moved across the stony slope once again. Progress slowed significantly, and their travel became quite tedious. Thankfully, as they made their way across the hill, they did not experience any more rockslides.

Once they left the rocky terrain behind them and entered the woods again, Prayerful hobbled over to a fallen log to rest.   They were all sore from the ordeal, and Prayerful, specifically, was in a lot of pain. Despite the ache in Prayerful's leg, they determined to only take a short break, for they needed to press on to find a more suitable place for the night.

As they talked of the possibility that his bone could be fractured, Prayerful became downcast. How could they continue on?   Their rate of travel had been greatly slowed, and he would also need time to heal. It would take much longer to reach their goal, especially if he had to stop frequently for breaks. He was frustrated, angry, depressed, and tempted to quit as he struggled holding back his tears. *How can the King allow such a thing to happen?* he wondered.

Eventually they got back up, and Steadfast helped Prayerful hobble along.   For the next several hours, they slowly progressed, taking occasional breaks for Prayerful. Though they tried to encourage him, he remained quite downcast and talked very little.   They were able to find a good place to camp that night, though Prayerful was often jolted awake by the sharp pain in his leg.

The next day, they descended into a beautiful valley and entered green pastureland. The level ground was a relief to Prayerful and slightly eased his discouragement. Traversing through the fields in this region, they passed by farms and fields and even came across a place where another road met the one they were on.   This valley certainly seemed very quiet and peaceful.

Later in the afternoon, as they ascended a slight knoll, Gentleness looked behind them and declared, "Someone is coming!"

Prayerful and Steadfast turned and gazed down the path on which they had just come. They saw two men leading a horse which was pulling a cartload of wares. Since it was about time for a break, they decided to wait for these merchants to catch up to them, hoping to find out information about any nearby town or village.

As the men drew closer, Prayerful noticed that, although they were dressed very well, they did not look gaudy or arrogant but rather joyful. Soon, the merchants pulled up alongside the place where the Pilgrims were sitting and stopped their cart.

"Hello," the older gentleman exclaimed.

"Good afternoon," Steadfast replied.

"You look like you had some kind of accident," the man stated as he observed their bandages.

"Yea, we had some trouble a little way back."

The older man asked with opened his arms, "Is there anything we can do to help?"

Prayerful sighed, "I don't know. We are just looking for a good place to spend the night."

"Several miles down the road is the Town of the Mind. That would be a good place to stay."

"Thank you," Prayerful replied.

The other man spoke up, "You know, we are heading to the Town of the Mind on some business. You could come with us."

"Yes," agreed the other man. "We would love to have your company."

"I would probably slow you down since I am having trouble walking," Prayerful said pointing to his left leg.

"That won't be a problem," the older man replied. "We have enough room in our wagon for you to ride."

"We don't want to be a bother," Steadfast stated.

"It is no bother at all. As we serve the Lord, we love to serve others," the man by the cart called out. "By the way, my name is Thinking Eternally, and this is my friend, Biblical Truth."

At Thinking Eternally's insistence, the three Pilgrims accepted the offer, and soon Prayerful was helped into the back of the two-wheeled cart. Since Gentleness and Steadfast had no trouble walking and there was no more room in the wagon, they decided to travel with Biblical Truth as he led the horse. Thinking Eternally chose to walk behind the cart so he could talk to Prayerful.

After they were going again, Thinking Eternally gestured toward Prayerful's injuries and asked, "So ... what happened?" Prayerful took the time to briefly explain their pilgrimage and concluded by describing the incident on the Hill of Testing.

"You are not the first who have been injured there," Thinking Eternally stated. "There have been a number of others who have taken The Path of Dedication. Sadly, most who travel through that hillside do end up getting hurt. A man, named Accuser, who does not like Pilgrims of the King, has a fort on the top of that hill. He intentionally throws the Rocks of Pain down the cliff in order to cause a landslide. His goal is to get the Pilgrims to fall and tumble to the bottom so he can criticize them before the Lord. He would love it if he could keep someone from going any further toward Near-to-God Mountain."

"Why does the King allow this?" Prayerful asked.

"No one likes to go through trials.... I certainly don't envy your predicament," Thinking Eternally said as he motioned once again toward Prayerful's leg. "But the King certainly knows what he is doing. Years ago, a man came through that hillside, and Accuser really worked hard to destroy his testimony. This man, who was known as a righteous man, had to endure five of the worst landslides I have ever heard of. He suffered many injuries, and it seemed like he lost everything he had — even his health. When his friends found him broken and bruised, they assumed that he had done something wrong and that God was judging him. As a result, they blamed him for his predicament. They assumed that he was being punished for some kind of sin, despite the fact he was innocent.

"Although this man didn't realize it, the King was testing his faith. He had to wrestle with the question: Would he keep going down The Path of Dedication, despite his pain and suffering? Thankfully, he remained faithful, and as a result, righteous Job passed the test. You see, sometimes God allows such hard times in our lives to test us, seeing if we will be faithful.

"The Lord also allows these things in our lives to help us grow stronger. I have observed that sometimes an injury such as yours, if you take care of it properly, will make you even stronger in the end." Prayerful's mind flashed back to his adventure with Believer when they were attacked by Sorrow and Suffering. He had been wounded in the attack and had battled some poisoning as a result. In the end, however, after the wound healed, that leg had become stronger than the other.

"Even if the injuries don't heal like we want, we can know God's strength in our lives. The more and more you realize how truly weak you are, the more you will be depending upon God to give you the strength you need. When you are weak, then you are truly strong in him.

"However, the *greatest* blessing in every trial is that you can know the depths of his love and grace in your life if you will let him. Paul said that he gloried in his infirmities that the power of Christ would rest upon him. Most people do not realize it, but these trials are more precious than gold, for through them, we get to know our Saviour in an even deeper way."

"I certainly do want to know him," Prayerful stated, "but how do I experience his grace through all this pain?"

"Do you see those walking sticks next to you on the cart?"

Prayerful looked to his left and spotted them.

"Take one. Consider it a gift."

Prayerful was hesitant to accept the merchant's generosity, but Thinking Eternally insisted. "This is the Staff of Dependance. You can use it as you press on in your journey. Even though you don't necessarily know *why* such difficulties happen, you must continue to trust that the Lord knows best. You must rest on his plan and submit to his will.

"Also, you must continue to have your focus on God. Try not to be consumed with your suffering, for then you will easily give up. Only by looking unto Jesus and remembering how he endured the cross, despising the shame, can we have the strength not to be weary and faint in our minds. He is our goal, and he must be our delight."

"I think I understand what you mean," Prayerful stated. "But I am in so much agony I don't know how I can do it."

"I understand," Thinking Eternally looked at him compassionately. "Time will help the pain, but remember this also … God wants you to know his peace even in the midst of suffering. Yes, we may be full of suffering in our body, but we can know a peace in our hearts. Ask God for help and continue to seek after him. He is always there to help us with our infirmities."

Prayerful certainly wanted to know the Lord's grace through this, but it was difficult. Not only did his leg and hand hurt, but he was overcome with discouragement at the tragic turn of events. He wanted to follow Thinking Eternally's advice and keep his eyes fixed upon his King, but it was not easy. He began to wonder if he would ever know peace again.

The Town of the Mind

As the cart jostled along the bumpy road, Prayerful grew more and more thankful for the company of their new friends. Watching the countryside pass by, Prayerful found that the words of the two merchants were full of comfort and wisdom, helping to ease his despair.

Thinking Eternally and Biblical Truth decided to take the Pilgrims to someone they knew who lived in the Town of the Mind. They described their old friend, Mr. Meditation, as being a very kind, wise, and hospitable man; they were sure he would welcome visitors for the night.

As they crested a grass-covered knoll, Prayerful caught his first glimpse of the Town of the Mind in the lush valley below. This home to a great number of people was perfectly nestled among the hills of the region, presenting a picturesque scene before them. The town itself, being relatively large, was protected by a great wall, making it appear strong and secure. Even from this distance, Prayerful could make out cranes and scaffolding which spoke of buildings currently under construction in this busy city.

As they entered through the gate, Prayerful was

amazed at the buzz of activity that filled the streets. People were constantly running from one place to another while others were working hard on various tasks. Cartloads of goods lined the streets as many merchants were in the middle of various business dealings. Prayerful's earlier observation of the construction was easily confirmed, for he could easily see that there were many areas in this town where new buildings were being erected.

Thinking Eternally explained that the town had several boroughs: Knowledge, Memory, Thinking, and Desires. The fact that these boroughs worked together under the leadership of the governor caused Prayerful to realize the complexity of this city. He also was intrigued by the various streets that they passed by. He observed Facts of God's Law, Wisdom, Goals, Selfish Desires, Readiness, Doubt, and so many more that he lost track of them all.

When they passed through the borough of Memory, Prayerful noticed that some of the buildings were neglected and seemed to be falling apart, but a majority of them were being utilized and were constantly kept in good repair. He also took note that the adjacent borough of Knowledge held a great, ever-expanding library.

They then entered the borough of Thinking where Meditation resided. Prayerful quickly found that this borough was so prominent that it often had messengers travel back and forth to the other areas in the city in order to accomplish business. In fact, Governor Will lived in Thinking, and he was in charge of everything that was done in the city. He oversaw the construction, trade, and defense of the city; at the same time, he also had to constantly judge the villains who sought to break the Law of the King. The more

Prayerful learned about this place, the more he realized that this town seemed to have a very detailed system of organization.

The two merchants soon turned onto Reflection Street, and before long, they stopped their cart in front of a large house. Prayerful was relieved that they had arrived, for by now, the jostling of the cart was beginning to amplify the pain in his leg.

Biblical Truth ascended the steps and knocked while everyone else waited. Much to everyone's surprise, Mr. Meditation came to the door within seconds as if he had been expecting them. Despite the man having white hair, Prayerful figured that he was middle aged. He certainly did appear quite friendly.

Meditation, immediately recognizing the merchants, welcomed everyone into his home. Biblical Truth and Thinking Eternally, however, politely refused, explaining that they had business in the city that needed their immediate attention. "But we were wondering," Thinking Eternally stated, "… would you be willing to take in these three Pilgrims? They have been on the road for weeks and have had a rough journey." Pointing to the back of the cart, he added, "Prayerful, here, got hurt and has quite a limp."

Meditation immediately stated, "Of course, they can stay here. I have several rooms ready for guests." Turning to the Pilgrims, he said, "Come on in."

"Thank you," Steadfast said with relief.

Meditation simply replied by nodding with a kind smile.

The Pilgrims said goodby to the merchants and thanked them for their kindness. Meditation then escorted his guests into his beautiful home and even offered a hand to help Prayerful as he limped up the outside steps. By now, the area around Prayerful's knee seemed to be quite swollen.

As they entered the home, Prayerful immediately noticed that pictures depicting Biblical scenes and verses of Scripture lined the walls. Meditation explained that he decorated in such a way so as to always draw his thoughts toward God. They quickly discovered that not only did he have quite a collection of art, but he also had a vast library filled with books that helped him dwell on eternity. He was a man who seemed to never rest his mind.

Since Prayerful was in no shape to converse, their host immediately led him to one of the guest rooms so he could get some rest. After Meditation made sure that all of his needs were met and they put a cool cloth on his swollen knee, Prayerful went to bed and fell into a deep sleep.

*   *   *

Prayerful hobbled along the hallway, leaning on the staff given to him by Thinking Eternally while he continually gazed around, observing the home. The mid-morning sunlight shone through the house, adding to the peaceful atmosphere. Despite the peace and comfort from this home, Prayerful remained somewhat downcast.

He found everyone in the sitting room and entered right when Gentleness asked their host, "Are you a musician?"

"Somewhat," he replied. "I can play both the harpsichord and violin. These other instruments that you see here are for my friends when they come to visit. You see, I love both playing *and* listening to music," he said with a smile.

Right when he finished speaking, Meditation

noticed Prayerful and got up to help him over to a comfortable seat across from his own chair.

"How are you doing?" Meditation asked once Prayerful was situated in his seat.

"I am still sore.... I can't put much weight on my leg."

"Well, you are welcome to stay here as long as you need. I will do what I can to help you."

"Thank you," Prayerful replied, not wanting to be a burden to anyone but thankful for the help.

They talked for a little while, and Prayerful quickly found out that Steadfast had already retold the story of their adventures. Soon, however, Prayerful's curiosity overcame him, and he shifted back to the previous conversation. "Have you always had such a great love for music?" he asked.

"Not really. Though I could play music since I was a child, I didn't really care much about it until several years ago. Before then, my life revolved around many other things." Meditation sat back in his chair as he began telling his story.

"I used to be a man with a wide variety of interests. I would collect all sorts of things ... anything that amused me. These items adorned my walls and filled my rooms. At first, many of these things seemed somewhat innocent, but then I began to want more, so I began purchasing stolen goods from a man named Lust. Mr. Violence also became one of my favorite sources of merchandise. Oddly enough, the authorities turned a blind eye to such actions.

"Anyway, I filled this place with all sorts of things that I now regret. Most people who passed by this beautiful house had no idea what it was truly like inside. They assumed that I was a good, respectable person in society...." Staring out the window he added,

"But I wasn't."

"What made you change?" Steadfast questioned.

"Really, I have to thank my close friend, Governor Will. When he went through The Change, many of the things I was doing were outlawed and strictly regulated. At first I fought these changes.... In fact, there were even a number of things that I tried to hide from the law. I won't bore you with the details, but it took a good bit of time before I gave in. However, let me tell you, I have never regretted doing so.

"Ever since then, I have been working to fill my house with things from the City of Scriptural Truth.... That is why Biblical Truth and Thinking Eternally are such good friends of mine," he added with a smile. "I knew that I needed to not just empty my house of the evil.... I needed to replace it with good."

After a sight pause, Prayerful asked, "You mentioned The Change. What do you mean by that?"

"I am sorry. I should have explained that better," Meditation stated as he leaned forward, resting his elbows on his knees. "To fully understand what I mean, you need to hear the history of this city, especially the story of Governor Will.... He has left quite a profound impact on this entire region.

"Years ago, when this town was first formed, Mr. Will was selected to be the Governor. He made a lot of mistakes, and he was constantly working to advance himself ... doing things for his own pleasure and popularity. The sad reality is that many in the Town of the Mind loved the choices he was making and helped him in any way they could.... They wanted to take part in his sin as well. The end result was that our small, young town grew very corrupt and full of evil. Very few outsiders knew how bad it was here.

"The Governor's head advisor, Mr. Sin Nature,

constantly prodded him to head the wrong direction. Sin Nature developed a massive building program, supposedly to enhance the lives of those who live in and around our town. Governor Will became actively involved with this, and thus many buildings of Evil Imaginations began springing up all over.

"In order to get everyone in the town to support this building program, the shops around the city were filled with the Merchandise of Unrighteousness, enticing everyone to seek evil. Governor Will accomplished this by developing good relations and trade agreements with the region of Carnality. At that time, the only road leading in and out of this area went straight to Carnality, and it eventually became a highway as traders went back and forth, buying and selling merchandise. The Governor loved the trade and often profited from it personally ... but things were about to change.

"One day, several years ago, a Pilgrim of the King came through here.... I think he was called Gospel Preacher.... Anyway, he began to speak against the evil and sin of our town. As I am sure you could guess, this caused quite a stir, and as a result, he was immediately arrested and brought before Governor Will to be judged. Sadly, this Pilgrim was banished from the region.

"Though the Governor did not like the truth that had been proclaimed, he was still bothered by what Gospel Preacher had said. Over the next several weeks, Governor Will talked to Sin Nature and declared his desire to curb the evil in the town. They began to put new paint on the buildings of sin, trying to cover up the evil; but it did not remove the problem. Eventually, they gave up.

"At that time, many did not realize that Gospel Preacher's friend, Voice of Admonition, was still in the city.   He began to speak out about sin, righteousness, and judgment, and he also preached how sin can be forgiven because of the death, burial, and resurrection of Christ. Governor Will couldn't banish him, for this man was not just a Pilgrim — he was the King's special messenger, … but he did try to silence him as much as possible. Well, Voice of Admonition continued speaking the truth as Will battled with what he knew was right. I am sure that if it weren't for the mercy of the King, Voice of Admonition would have left … maybe for good.

"As he kept on preaching, Governor Will slowly softened and began to listen. Within time, he eventually broke and repented of the sin and evil that he had done. He called upon the Lord and trusted the promises of the King that Christ would save him from his sin. That was the beginning of a new era for us.   Because of his repentance, there were many changes that took place in town."

"Is that what you were meaning with 'The Change?'" Prayerful questioned for clarification.

"Yes. You see, there were a number of immediate changes; others took time. One of the first was that the King sent someone to live here permanently.   He is known as Comforter and is a very powerful and wise individual who constantly encourages Governor Will to do right.

"Another change was that the Governor began to submit to the Law of the King. This, of course, is when things began to impact me," Meditation commented, referring to his own personal story.

"Well, our commerce was effected as well.   We opened a new trade route with another nearby city, Scriptural Truth.   Consequently, over time, we have imported more and more goods from there and less merchandise from Carnality. Since the Governor is the one directly in control of trade, my desire is that he will one day lock the gates heading toward Carnality once and for all, … but even now, he still allows them to be opened.

"Why doesn't he stop trading with that city?" Prayerful asked.

"It is a battle for him since both of his advisors, Sin Nature and Comforter, are totally opposite. Sin Nature only seeks for those things from Carnality, but Comforter encourages him to buy righteous things from Scriptural Truth. Thus, the Governor has to choose who to listen to. He knows what is right but doesn't always do it."

Meditation paused the conversation as he stood up and announced that he would bring in tea for everyone. Prayerful was thankful for this break, for he needed time to digest what they had just been told. While they were waiting for their host to return, Prayerful continually replayed the story in his mind, trying to comprehend everything that had taken place in this city.

In a few minutes, Meditation returned with the hot beverage and served his guests. Everyone took a few moments to sip their tea before they resumed the conversation. Prayerful, being fully engrossed in the story, was the first to speak.

"You mentioned that there were some changes in the Town of the Mind that took some time. What were they?" he asked.

After a slight pause, Meditation replied, "I guess you could simply say that Comforter has been working on rebuilding our town. You see, the old buildings designed by Sin Nature are built poorly — they were designed contrary to the King's building code, and thus they have many problems. All such buildings are structurally weak and are very dark, becoming easy hideouts for evil. The Governor is often amazed when Comforter points out various buildings that are full of sin.… He had no idea how bad things truly were here.

"Thankfully, Comforter already knows all of the structures in town, and he is slowly and carefully tearing down the buildings of sin and constructing ones of righteousness. He is a skilled engineer who takes his time and does things right. He wants lasting results.

"Sadly, There have been certain structures that Governor Will has fought Comforter on. Comforter has had to work with him for quite a while before the Governor would relent on such projects."

Meditation took a few moments to sip his cooling tea. "Oh, I almost forgot," he suddenly announced. "There is another change that has happened here. Comforter has also planted an orchard. It may seem trivial, but this has allowed the town to produce the Fruits of Righteousness. The fruit has become a valuable commodity, impacting both the town and the region around us."

"Interesting," Prayerful commented. "It certainly sounds like Comforter has done a lot already."

"The changes have *definitely* been good, even though some here still want to follow Sin Nature. I think that Governor Will would do well to seek even more trade from Scriptural Truth and continue to minimize trade from Carnality. After all, what you allow through the gates is what the town will become.

A Special Visit

Throughout the rest of the day, Prayerful was able to rest some more, but during this time, he began to dwell on his misfortune. Specifically, he began to think about what would happen if he had to delay the journey until his leg was completely healed. His heart sank at such a thought, for depending how bad the injury was, he could be there for quite some time. *What about my mission?*

Throughout the afternoon, he grew more depressed, his mind continually dwelling on such thoughts. Though the others tried to encourage him, he would not be comforted. By the time that the sun was setting, Prayerful felt exhausted and weak. He figured that he was still worn out from the events of the last few days, and thus he went to bed early.

After he laid down, however, he found it impossible to fall asleep. He tossed and turned restlessly. Adding to this discomfort, his back ached, and he vacillated between shivering and sweating. After suffering miserably for hours, he finally dozed off late into the night.

*   *   *

Prayerful heard the knocking on his door and struggled to open his eyes. "Prayerful, are you alright?" Steadfast's voice filtered through the door. Prayerful only groaned in response; he was miserable and exhausted. Steadfast cracked open the door and repeated, "Are you ok?"

Prayerful simply shook his head, feeling too weak and sore to speak. Beads of perspiration ran down Prayerful's forehead as Steadfast entered and came near his bedside.

"You don't look good at all," Steadfast stated.

Prayerful looked up at his friend and whispered, "I didn't sleep much last night … and I feel like I have a fever."

"I better get Meditation and see what we can do for you."

Steadfast left and in a few minutes returned with the older man. They brought a bowl of cool water and a cloth to help cool him down. Steadfast soaked the cloth in the water, and then placed it on Prayerful's head while Meditation watched. The damp cloth only helped ease his discomfort a little.

After several minutes of silence, Meditation declared, "I think I am going to ask my friend, Dr. Understanding, to come look at you…. You are in pretty rough shape."

Prayerful, though remaining silent, was grateful. He hoped that the doctor would provide some answers, not only for the fever but also for his other injuries. By now, the pain in his leg had dissipated some, but his knee still throbbed.

After Meditation went to get the doctor and Steadfast left him alone to rest, Prayerful fell into great despondency. *Why does this sort of thing have to happen to me? … Especially as I am on a mission for the King.* He was so depressed that he began to lose all desire to finish his journey. He wanted to go home.

Prayerful struggled with discouragement for the next hour while he waited. Steadfast occasionally checked in on him, bringing him food and water. Prayerful, however, only took a couple sips of the cool liquid and did not attempt to eat.

Right after the clock in the hall struck noon, Meditation entered the room followed by a stocky, balding man carrying a black bag. This was Dr. Understanding. The physician took Prayerful's temperature and ran through several other tests while he listened to Prayerful's story. He then took a look at the cut on Prayerful's hand, and spent some time inspecting the injured leg.

After he was finished with the examination, the doctor declared, "You have a bad case of the Fever of Despair. I have found that those who go through hard times often battle this disease and are ready to give up." Prayerful stared off into the distance as he listened to the physician.

"I have some medicine that will help you, but you need to listen carefully and follow my instructions. There were some patients of mine who had this fever and were so discouraged that they never took their medication. As you can guess, they never fully got over the disease. Please follow my instructions carefully, and don't give up no matter how long it takes.

"I am going to leave two different types of medicine for you. Before every meal you need to take a spoonful of Eternal Focus. Then after you eat, take a spoonful of Hope in God. Most importantly, you need to drink a lot of the Water of the Word. This sickness can be difficult to conquer … and it will take time, but the more water you drink, the sooner the fever will break."

The doctor placed the bottles of medicine on a nearby dresser as Meditation declared that he would make sure that the doctor's orders were followed faithfully.

Prayerful was afraid to ask, but he had to know the truth. "How is my leg?" he questioned

"It looks like you suffered quite a bad blow. The good news is that the boulder hit you in such a way that it didn't break any bones. The area below your left knee has been bruised quite badly, but it seems to be healing well. The problem is with your knee itself. Evidently, when you were hit, your knee took the brunt of the impact." The doctor paused and shook his head slowly as he stared at the back wall. "I have seen injuries like this before." Looking straight into Prayerful's eyes, he said, "I can't guarantee that it will heal fully."

"Do you mean I might never walk again?" Prayerful asked as fear filled his heart. He was prepared for bad news — but not this.

"I certainly would like to say that it will fully heal without any permanent results; but it is more likely that you will have some kind of limp the rest of your life."

Doctor Understanding gazed at Prayerful with compassionate eyes, but Prayerful stared blankly out a nearby window — this news was certainly not what he wanted to hear. Even after further questioning, the doctor insisted that there was nothing more he could do to help it heal properly. Prayerful just needed to continue to rest and stay off his feet as much as possible.

Prayerful thanked the doctor for his help though he was more discouraged now than before. After Meditation and Doctor Understanding left, various thoughts plagued Prayerful's mind. *How can I take a journey for the Lord now? How would I be able to stand in the middle of a battle ... especially if I am surrounded by enemies? ... How can I deliver the sword?* Then, a dreaded word burst into his mind: *Crippled.* In the solitude of his room, Prayerful wept.

The next several days were quite a battle for Prayerful. Though his friends tried to make sure he took his medicine and spoke encouraging words to him, he continued to battle the Fever of Despair.

Five days later, the fever finally broke. The doctor allowed him to get up and move around a little; however, he found this difficult with the lingering pain in his knee. By now, he could put a little weight on it, but he continually walked with a limp. Fearing that his knee was not mending, he began praying that it would heal completely — how else could he go on? Certainly the Lord would not allow this to be permanent, especially since he still had an assignment to complete.

Prayerful began to pass his days by reading the Scriptures and praying. Consequently, the desire to climb Near-to-God Mountain rekindled in his heart. Though the flame of longing was small, it grew day by day. He wanted to go on. Though progress with his knee was slow, Prayerful convinced himself that he would soon be healed completely.

A week later, the rest of Prayerful's injuries were healed; however, his knee still had a dull ache while he walked. Upon further examination, the doctor thought that it might heal a little more, but, ultimately, he declared that Prayerful would have a limp the rest of his life. The damage was permanent.

Prayerful could not understand why God would allow this to happen. He had a mission to fulfill — how could he go on as a cripple? Deep within his heart, he knew that the King had some purpose behind this injury — even if he never found out what it was. Despite this, he struggled for several days, battling anger and frustration. Eventually, Prayerful resigned himself to life with this disability. Figuring he could not continue on with his journey, he had no idea what he should do next. The only thing he could think to do was to pray.

*   *   *

The shade of the tree provided a wonderful reprieve from the burning sun. Prayerful was glad that he could get some time outside after being cooped up in the house so long. Meditation's large botanical garden behind his home was the perfect spot to quietly enjoy some fresh air.

A slight breeze blew some dried leaves around his feet as Prayerful found a small bench and sat down to think. He sighed as a battle raged inside his heart. Tears once again came to his eyes as he thought, *I wish I could make it all the way up Near-to-God Mountain! I wish I could have another chance to pick up the sword of the Lord and stand for my King.... It looks like such things are now impossible.* He bowed his head in regret, dwelling upon his weakness, wondering what the King wanted from him now.

At that moment, he heard the door to the house creak open, followed by the sound of the latch clicking shut again. Prayerful figured that either Steadfast or Meditation wanted to join him, but he was not sure if he wanted company at that moment. He kept his eyes on a nearby lily as he heard the approaching footsteps.

"May I join you?" a strong, but gentle voice asked.

In surprise, Prayerful snapped his head up and

beheld the man before him. This stranger seemed to have an aura of royalty, yet, strangely enough, he was somewhat familiar.

"I am Comforter," the man said. "I know all about your journey, and I wanted to talk with you." Prayerful instantly remembered Meditation's story about the Town of the Mind and how Comforter was sent from the King to bring about many changes in this city. Prayerful was shocked that such an important and busy man would take time to meet with him.

Comforter sat next to Prayerful and asked, "Why are you downcast?"

After a short moment, Prayerful answered, "Every beat of my heart cries out to continue on with the journey the King gave me, but it looks like I will live the rest of my life with a limp. There is no way I can continue on...."

"Hope in God; he is the health of your countenance. You don't have to fear, for in your distress, you have called upon God, and he has heard you. He still wants you to press toward the mark."

"I don't know if I can go on," Prayerful stammered as he shook his head. A moment later, a thought came to him, and instantly hope swelled up in his heart. Locking eyes with Comforter, he enthusiastically asked, "Will the King heal me so I can keep going?!"

Comforter looked compassionately into his eyes and said, "Paul had a thorn in the flesh and prayed that it be removed from him, but God let it stay, helping him remain humble. This thorn of yours is to constantly remind you of your need to depend upon God, for it is very easy for Pilgrims to rest on their own strength and accomplishments instead of their King."

"But how can I climb the steep slopes like this?

How can I face the enemies of my Lord with a poor leg?" Prayerful questioned, rubbing his left knee.

"Walk by faith, not by sight. God's grace is sufficient for you, for his strength is made perfect in weakness. When the way is too steep, call upon him, for he is your strength and song. Also, when you are beset by your foes round about, call upon the Lord who is worthy to be praised. This is how you will be saved from your enemies."

Prayerful sat in silence, trying to soak in all of this while being plagued with doubt. He certainly wanted to keep going, but he did not like the idea of continuing on with his limp.

Reading his thoughts, Comforter explained, "You need to present your body a living sacrifice. Your desires, dreams, goals, ambitions, and anything else that you hold dear must be handed over to the King. Although your flesh hates it, God longs that you give everything completely to Him and follow His way whole-heartedly. Self must be out of the picture. Only then will you truly be able to accomplish the plan of the Lord. For when you are weak, then are you truly strong."

Prayerful was beginning to understand what Comforter was saying. Deep down inside, he wanted to give everything over to the Lord, yet it was a great struggle to do so. How could he give up some of the things that he counted most dear to him — even his own health? How could he get himself out of the picture? In his heart, he knew the answer: he had to make the choice of surrender every day.

"There is something else that is very important," Comforter added. "As you get your eyes off yourself, you must set your focus on the King. Abide in him. Daily spend time with him, meditating in his Law day and night. Pray without ceasing. You will find that as you rely on him for strength and grace, you will know him in a way that you have never known him before."

Despite his reservation, a shiver ran up Prayerful's spine at the renewed hope of knowing the King. There was nothing that he longed for more than to walk with the Lord closely. Right then, Prayerful determined that he, with God's help, would seek to keep self out of the picture so that he would know his Master in an even greater way. If this meant suffering in pain for the rest of his life, so be it.

"I want to follow my Savior wherever he will lead me," Prayerful voiced his heart's decision.

"It will not be easy," Comforter said, "but the trial of your faith is more precious than the gold that perishes; — it will be worth it all." Comforter smiled and placed his hand on Prayerful's shoulder. "You are not too far from Near-to-God Mountain. Keep going no matter what the cost, for the greatest treasure is to know the King.   Also, don't forget, the sword must be placed in the hands of the one who is called to bear it."

These few minutes that Prayerful spent with Comforter renewed the vision of his task for the King. This time, however, he had an even greater longing to reach his goal. The thirst to be near to the Lord grew in his bosom until it was an unquenchable longing. He would set out as soon as possible. For the first time in many days, joy and gladness overflowed his heart. Even after Comforter left, Prayerful felt like singing.

The Ancient Museum

The fresh air and sunny sky felt good to Prayerful as he and his friends trekked along the grassy path. Even though he would finish his journey with this limp, he was thankful to be on the road again. Much to his surprise, he did not have to stop very often for a break. He could clearly tell that God was giving him strength to press on.

They left the Town of the Mind a day ago, and the pathway once again had a new name. It was now called the Trail of Love.

As they journeyed along, Prayerful thought of Passionate for Truth's sword hanging at his side, waiting to be handed over to the next one who will carry it in the name of the King. The thrill of his mission once again drew him to a deeper appreciation for the Lord who had called him to this task. *Why would the King choose such a weak man for this job?* He could never figure out the answer.

Love for the King filled his very being, consuming his thoughts. When he saw the trees, he remembered how he needed to be rooted and grounded in Christ. The birds flying through the sky above reminded him to wait upon the Lord and he would mount up with wings as eagles. Beholding nearby fruit trees, he thought of the importance of abiding in Christ to bear much fruit. Everything he saw, heard, and smelled drew him to meditate upon God.

As his thoughts were elevated to the throne above, his soul rejoiced in God his Savior. His heart carried a song that occasionally would flow out from his lips; his love for the Lord and the joy in his heart were irreplaceable. Especially after his meeting with Comforter, he longed to spend even more time with the Lord, and thus he prayed often.

The trio continued on and soon entered the Slopes of Supplication. Although there were a good number of difficult hills to ascend, they were thrilled to be climbing them, for they knew that these slopes were part of the foothills of Near-to-God Mountain. They were getting close to their goal.

For the next several days, they hiked along the mountain trail, often stopping to pray and sing. One morning, as they crested a particularly steep hill, they stood for a moment, staring down the path ahead. A quarter mile away, a large, three-storied structure stood like an island resting on a small plain in this hilly landscape.

As they approached the great wooden building, they saw a man sweeping the outside walk in front of the main entrance. This man, though appearing to be one of the oldest men that Prayerful had ever seen, seemed to be quite strong and fit. His long, white beard and wrinkled face were quite a contrast to his erect, muscular frame.

"Hello," Prayerful called out.

"Good morning," the old man replied with a voice that exuded strength. "Welcome to the Museum of Answered Prayer. I am Intercessor."

At the mention of the name of this place, all three friends immediately had their interest peaked.

"The Museum of Answered Prayer ..." Steadfast repeated. "Do you mind if we could see what you have inside?"

"I would love to show you around," Intercessor said. "Come on in." He led them to the front door and held it open for his three guests. As Prayerful entered the museum, he saw a sign above the door which read, "Ask and receive that your joy may be full."

After everyone was inside, Intercessor explained, "As you look around, you will find that there is a mixture of art and various artifacts here. Each item is a reminder of the many prayers that God has already answered." Entering into a great room that spanned the majority of the first floor, Intercessor added, "This first floor contains items from the prayers that were answered during Bible times."

They began meandering throughout the room, examining various artifacts and soaking in the information. Looking around, Prayerful recognized Gideon's fleece, the iron bars reminiscent of Peter's miraculous escape from prison, various paintings from Abraham, Isaac, and Jacob, and many other such things. He also noted that there were several sections for the answered prayers of Moses, Joshua, and Daniel. It did not take long before Prayerful became overwhelmed at the great number of things that lined the walls and filled the tables.

"Could you explain this one to me?" Gentleness asked Intercessor. She pointed to a picture of a woman gazing up to heaven with tears running down her face while a priest was standing nearby.

"That is a scene in the life of Hannah," Intercessor explained. "She was barren and wanted a son more than anything, so she came to the Tabernacle and poured out her heart before the Lord. In fact, she was so overcome with her burden that the priest, Eli, thought she was drunk. In the end, God granted her request and gave her a son: Samuel." After a pause, Intercessor added, "I guess what I love the most about the story of Hannah is that it reminds me that I need to pray with tears.

"The exciting thing is that her son also learned the preciousness of prayer. If you look on the shelf next to the painting of Hannah, you will see a great number of artifacts from the life of Samuel. Do you see that large stone?" Intercessor asked, pointing to Samuel's shelf.

"Yes."

"That is Ebenezer Rock which Samuel set up after Israel won a great victory over the Philistines. Samuel fought that battle on his knees rather than with a sword in his hand. The victory through prayer was so significant that God's hand was against the Philistines all the days of Samuel. It is amazing that almost every time we read of Samuel, he is talking to the Lord. He was a faithful man who is considered one of the greatest men of prayer in all of Israel's history."

After several more minutes of looking around, Steadfast called out, "I see that you have a stone from Nehemiah's wall."

"Yes, I nicknamed it *The Impossible Stone.* Everyone thought that the wall could never be built, and thus they lived lives of defeat. Nehemiah, however, had a vision of what God could do. He prayed for several months about the problem, and, eventually, the wall was built in just fifty-two days!"

"What makes this account even more precious is that God made it possible that Nehemiah, himself, could be the very one to build the wall," Prayerful added.

"The greatest blessing of all is that a revival broke out in Israel as a result," Intercessor continued. "Both a physical and a spiritual work were accomplished because one man begged God to do the impossible."

When they were finished looking around in this first room, Intercessor led them up a flight of stairs. As they entered the room on the next floor, Interpreter declared, "Here you will find only a *small* sampling of the answers to prayer that people saw *after* the Bible was completed. I love this room because sometimes we can get the attitude that people in Scripture were extra special and that such wonderful things cannot happen today. This room reminds us that God answers prayer throughout *all* time."

As Prayerful glanced around, he could barely see any open space on the walls or tables. Artifacts and paintings were everywhere, and soon everyone was scattered among the various exhibits.

Prayerful found that he could recognize a few names, such as George Muller and Hudson Taylor, but most of the things in the room spoke of the vast number of unknown Christians who saw God work in mighty ways through prayer. Paintings depicting old-time revivals lined the walls on the left. Bandages and other medical supplies were reminders that God healed people from diseases while baskets of bread displayed how God had provided food to those in need. There was so much to see.

As Prayerful moved to a display on the right hand wall, he was a little confused, for on the table in front of him sat a bottle of water with no explanation as to its significance. Prayerful asked, "What is this?"

"That bottle of water represents the many times

that God has altered the weather patterns for those who prayed. Multiple stories could be told of a storm that was approaching and Pilgrims getting on their knees, begging God to hold off the rain. Then, they would watch as the wall of rain stopped and went around them. Sometimes the homes and buildings all around their location were drenched, but they were completely dry." He then added, "Unfortunately, I cannot display every answer to prayer that God has ever given.... This place would not be able to contain it all."

After another minute, Steadfast, who was on the other side of the room, stated, "This is an interesting one." Prayerful turned and saw him at the George Muller display, reading a plaque in front of an old brick. "It says here that one day, one of the boilers in his children's home sprung a leak. The weather was cold, and it would have taken several days to make the repair because the boiler was bricked in. Muller prayed that the weather would change and that the repairmen would have a mind to work. The very day that work began, the weather grew warmer, making it unnecessary to heat the buildings, and then the men worked for thirty-six hours straight in order to finish the job."

"I never heard about that," Prayerful remarked.

"If you look around, you will notice that there is no limit to the ways that God can work," Intercessor commented. "People have received answers for safety, wisdom ... strength ... health, and much more. In the far corner, there is a display with various tools showing how God answered the prayers of those needing help with various projects. There is another exhibit with items that had been lost but were found with God's help. The painting at the back of the room shows how the Lord has brought thoughts and ideas to people when they needed wisdom. There is no end to what our

God can do in answer to prayer."

Everyone continued looking around at the artifacts, but after a few more minutes, Gentleness asked another question, "What is this book? It is huge and seems to be filled with a list of names." She was examining one of the largest printed works that Prayerful had ever seen; it was tall, wide, and thick.

"That is a book recording the names of people who were saved as a result of someone praying for them. Sometimes the prayer warrior would spend years and even decades on his knees praying for the salvation of a loved one. Although each person has to make their own decision for salvation, God certainly can do a great work in the heart in answer to prayer."

Soon Intercessor led them to another set of stairs heading to the third floor. As Prayerful hobbled up the steps, he was a taken aback by the fact that either side of the stairway was lined with mirrors. He did not understand the reason for them at first, and the sign above his head did little to alleviate his confusion, for it merely declared: The Stairway of Mirrors. However, the purpose of these mirrors quickly became evident.

Prayerful glanced at the mirror to his right and saw something that he did not expect. Rather than seeing his own image, he beheld a scene from his journey with Believer. Prayerful watched as he saw the two of them at the Crossroads of Decision. They had not known where they should go, so they prayed asking for direction. The scene in the mirror moved quickly, and he watched how God answered their prayer by sending Godly Advice and his wife to direct them.

The mirror then changed to display another event in his life. It showed how Help was sent after they prayed during their attempt to rescue Half-Heart from Covetous' dungeon. After that scene, other events appeared, reminding Prayerful of various answers to prayer that he had received in his life.

He eventually glanced up the stairs at everyone else and found that they too had their eyes glued to the mirrors as his friends were also being reminded of their own prayers that God had answered. Prayerful was struck with the thought, *I wonder how much truly could be done if we were on our knees in prayer even more?*

After several minutes, everyone pealed their eyes off these Mirrors of Reflection and climbed the rest of the way up the stairs. Entering into this third room, Prayerful was quite surprised at how different it was from what they had already seen. In the middle of the room stood a large table with a great number of unopened gifts. After looking at the presents for several moments, Prayerful glanced around and grew even more mystified. The bare walls and empty shelves made it seem that this room was not yet finished.

"There are several things you need to understand here," Intercessor began. "First of all, those gifts on the table will never be opened. The Lord has been willing to grant many requests throughout all of time, but not all requests have been answered. These presents were prepared to be given, but Christians never received them for various reasons."

"Why not?" Gentleness wondered.

"Well, sometimes the request is simply not God's plan for them. He knows what is best and will at times say, 'no' to a particular request. Often, however, the Lord will not answer a specific prayer because when one regards iniquity in his heart, the Lord will not hear him. God will also not answer a request that is asked when we want to consume it upon our lusts.... Also, there are times that we don't ask in faith. However, I believe that one of the biggest reasons why many prayers have not been answered is something else."

"What is it?" Gentleness asked.

"People give up," Intercessor declared with a slight edge of frustration as he threw his hands into the air. "We are commanded to pray without ceasing, yet there are many who quit. We grow tired of praying.... We lose faith.... We get busy and forget the need.... Sometimes we even assume that God will answer 'No,' and thus we give up. These unopened gifts are a reminder to never quit." Intercessor let his words sink in for a moment. "So, the point is this, you need to keep on praying until the Lord gives you a clear answer, whether it is a 'yes' or a 'no.'

"This leads to the other thing that I want you to notice about this room. Those empty shelves are waiting to be filled. God is the same yesterday, today, and forever. He is the one who delights in hearing his people cry out to him, and he still moves when we pray." Intercessor went on, his eyes beginning to burn with excitement with each word, "So many people have no idea of the true potential behind prayer. Although our words are feeble at best, the King is great and mighty — he is the one that accomplishes the work. He is still the King of Kings and Lord of Lords who rules upon his throne. The potential of prayer is as great as our Lord, himself.

"Many Pilgrims in the past have taken up the mantle of prayer and saw great and mighty things accomplished. The question I often ask myself is: Who will take up that mantle today? Remember, the eyes of the Lord are upon the righteous, and his ears are open to their cry. He will answer even though things may seem impossible.

"The sad reality is that today so many have neglected prayer. They are too entangled with the affairs of this life that they don't want to take time with God.… And whenever they do pray, it is more of a ritual than actually enjoying time with God." Intercessor sighed and shook his head. "If Christ had to spend all night in prayer, why do we think we can get by with just a few minutes a day? Imagine what could happen if Pilgrims today would recognize how important and great prayer truly is; I am sure that the world itself could be greatly impacted by it!" He paused again as he stared out a nearby window, his mind deep in thought, while everyone else stood in silence, contemplating his challenge.

After a minute of silence, Intercessor turned his attention back to the group. "I have one more room for you to see." Leading them through the doorway and across the hall, he stated, "This next room is the most important one in this entire building."

As soon as Intercessor opened the door, Prayerful's mouth dropped open, for it seemed like he was in an entirely different building. Rather than being a space filled with a collection of various artifacts, this room was ornately decorated like the throne room of a palace. Marble pillars lined the outside edges while all around the room, various Biblical names for God were etched with gold into the walls. The great throne itself stood at the far end of the room upon a pedestal with seven steps leading up to it and a red carpet stretching from the doorway to the foot of the throne. Right before the steps, a golden picture of the altar of incense was stitched into the red fabric.

Prayerful immediately understood what this room represented. Christians can come boldly before the throne of God so that any request can be brought before the Lord. Everyone was silent as the wonder of prayer overwhelmed them all.

Intercessor soon looked everyone straight in the eye and said, "The greatest part of prayer is that we are spending time with the One who created us. It is more than just bringing requests.... It is knowing Him in a personal relationship. Nothing ... nothing is more precious than knowing God. It is an amazing wonder that God, who is so high and exalted, is willing to know and spend time with sinful man. You need to remember this: those who have walked closest to our Savior and knew Him deeply were people who would spend hours on their knees."

At these words, Prayerful's heart cried out with a burning passion, *Oh, that I might know him!* Then, another longing began to grow in Prayerful's heart. *Since God is the same yesterday, today, and forever, why aren't we seeing Him do great things through prayer today?*

"I can see by the look in your eyes that you want the King to accomplish mighty works through your prayers," Intercessor said to Prayerful.

"Yes ... I do," Prayerful answered, a little amazed at the insight that this man had. "I am afraid that I have become content praying only for small things when God has so much more that He wants to do."

"That is good for you to have such a desire. Many Pilgrims imagine that the great answers to prayer are *only* things of the past."

After a moment of pause, Prayerful replied, "God has not changed — we have. We have forgotten that all things whatsoever we ask in prayer believing, we will receive, and that all things are possible to the one who believes."

"Right," Intercessor agreed. "As you examine Scripture, you will notice that it is the rare exception for God to refuse someone's request. God has answered many prayers throughout all of time...." After a moment of thought he added, "Since you are seeking to step out in faith and see God work, I have something to give you."   Intercessor reached down to his belt and unfastened a small leather pouch. He opened the sack, pulled out a tiny wooden box, and handed it to Prayerful. Although the box was small enough to fit within the palm of his hand, it was full of intricate carvings that displayed a great throne and a crown on its lid.

"The box is nothing compared to the treasure within," Intercessor explained, prodding Prayerful to open the little container.

As he slowly lifted the lid, his eyes shifted from the dark sea of velvet lining the interior, to the sole item that was contained within. Prayerful was immediately dumbfounded — how could the tiny object he was gazing at be so valuable. Inside the box lay the smallest seed that Prayerful had ever seen.

"This is the mustard seed called Faith," Intercessor explained.   "God desires us to always depend upon Him and to believe His promises, even if He does tell us 'No.'   It may seem small, but don't discount what the Lord can do with little things. Because of the power of our King, this mustard seed has the potential to move mountains.   It is yours if you choose to take it."

"I will…. Thank you," Prayerful said as he closed the lid to this treasure.

"Give your thanks to the King who has given us His promises.   Now, don't forget to use it…. Some have," Intercessor stated as he handed Prayerful the leather pouch to keep the box in.

Although Prayerful knew that the Lord could do exceedingly abundantly above all that he could ask or even think, he truly had no idea how God would work through this seed of Faith.

183

Searching for the One

As Prayerful, Steadfast, and Gentleness crested a particularly tall hill, they stopped and gazed at the scene ahead. The cluster of houses in the distance indicated that they were near their destination. When they had said goodby to Intercessor three days ago, he told them that the Trail of Love would lead to the Town of Faithful Christianity which was nestled among the great hills at the base of Near-to-God Mountain. This town was only a few miles ahead, standing out against the backdrop of this great mountain range.

The few scattered homes in the distance hardly could be accounted for as a town, but there was no denying that this was Faithful Christianity. Prayerful's heart leapt for joy at the thought that this stage of his journey was so near its end. He even wondered if the one who was to bear the sword lived in this village.

The weary travelers glanced at one another and gave a relieved smile, for although they had enjoyed their time in the mountain range, they were ready to rest their sore feet. They were far enough up into the mountains that there were no trees, and the grass above them soon gave way to the rocky surface of the mountain. A short hill rose to their right, along which their trail ran, and a few hundred yards to their left, the slope plummeted downward toward the lower hills below.

Prayerful took a few moments to gaze at the scenery around them, never growing tired of seeing its beauty. The view to the left was especially stunning, for the land stretched out before them as far as the eye could see. All shades of greens, blues, and purples painted one of the most picturesque scenes that Prayerful had ever beheld.

Suddenly, Gentleness declared, "There is a man over there, sitting next to that big rock."

Prayerful's eyes gazed over to where a prominent boulder rested a few feet from the edge of the hill on their left. At its base, sat a man with his traveling bag in the grass and his staff resting against the stone. He was leaning forward with his elbows on his knees while gazing out across the valleys. He was so intent that it appeared he was looking for something.

"We haven't seen too many people the last week or so," Steadfast commented quietly.

"Well, let's go talk to him and see what we can learn," Prayerful declared as he began trudging over to the man.

"It isn't everyday that we see someone this high in the mountains," Prayerful called out to the stranger when they only a few yards away.

"Oh!" the man screamed, jumping at the sound of Prayerful's voice. He put his hand over his heart and then took a deep breath saying, "You startled me…. I didn't see you coming."

"We are sorry…. We didn't mean to scare you," Gentleness apologized.

"That's ok. I guess I was just so lost in thought that I wasn't paying attention to anything around me. I am Look-Back," the man declared, standing up and introducing himself.

"I am Prayerful. And this is Steadfast and his wife, Gentleness.... You have certainly chosen a beautiful spot on which to sit."

"It certainly is," Look-Back agreed as he turned to take another look across the valleys. "So, are you Pilgrims as well?" he added, bringing his gaze back to them.

"We are," Prayerful affirmed.

"So am I. You must be on your way to the Town of Faithful Christianity.... After all, that is where this road ends," he stated, pointing back at the Trail of Love. "I was on my way there when I stopped at this spot about a week ago."

Prayerful paused for a second, and then asked, "Why did you stop?"

"Well ... a friend encouraged me to come along with him on this journey to the mountain, and I traveled with him for many weeks, facing all sorts of dangers. By the time we got here, I decided it was time for me to take a break. You see, I miss my old home and my former life ... and from here I have been able to spot villages, towns, and even the City of Vanity. These sights remind me of home. I really enjoy spending time reminiscing about the good times I had down there."

The three friends were a little shocked at this.

"Instead of looking down there, you need to look up to Near-to-God Mountain — having your eyes fixed on the Author and Finisher of your faith. He is the only thing worth seeking," Steadfast declared.

"Well, I am glad you want to go further, but that is just not for me. Besides, I think God is pleased with what I have done already, so why should I do more?" Looking back over the valley he added, "Honestly, I

think I would just rather live the life that I had before….
It certainly was much easier," Look-Back reasoned.

"No one who has put his hand to the plough and looks back is fit for the Kingdom of God," Prayerful stated. "Besides, we should not be like the children of Israel who longed to return to Egypt after they had been set free. Rather, God wants us to exercise ourselves unto godliness."

"I think your idea of godliness is for those who are extreme," Look-Back retorted, growing a little annoyed as he turned and glared at Prayerful. "I *do* think it is important to be good … but you don't have to necessarily be some great holy man. As long as I live a moral and honest life, work hard at the task I am given, and go to church, then that is all that matters."

"But that would mean you missed the ultimate goal," Steadfast replied. "Paul longed to know *Him*," he said, pointing toward the mountain, "and we should too. We need to *forsake* all and follow Christ."

Look-Back turned his gaze back down to the valleys below and simply shook his head and huffed in frustration.

"Remember Lot's wife," Steadfast warned. Then without another word, he turned about and began trudging up the trail again; Prayerful and Gentleness quickly joined him, for Look-Back, clearly, would not listen. Once they were on the road again, Steadfast gazed off into the distance and said, "It won't be long before Look-Back decides to not just live on memories — he will return to the things he loves and forget about truly knowing the King."

*　　*　　*

The Town of Faithful Christianity was not very

188

populated. In fact, when the three friends entered the village, it appeared that there were a number of older houses that had been abandoned. However, in the very center of the town stood a beautifully well-maintained church surrounded by a good number of occupied homes. Though this town seemed to be only a shadow of its former glory, it still gave a peaceful welcome to the weary travelers.

After entering the village, the three friends walked along the main street, passing by a number of homes and an occasional pedestrian. Soon they came to a small general store, and they all agreed to stop. They figured that this would be the best place to learn more about this town — and maybe find a place to stay.

As they entered into the store, a woman came out from the back room and stood on the other side of the counter. The three travelers made their way to her and introduced themselves. They then asked the woman to tell them about Faithful Christianity.

The clerk, named Mrs. Righteous, took a deep breath, and then said, "Many people have come here who are seeking the Lord and have made this place of faithfulness their home. I would say that most of the folks here are spiritually-minded people, and I am sure that as *you* seek to walk with the Lord, you will find close fellowship with them. Everyone here knows the Word of God and daily feasts on the strong meat of Scripture.... They also enjoy milk once in a while, too," she added with a smile.

As she was finishing her sentence, a stout, balding man came out from the back room, carrying a parchment and quill. Evidently, he was in the middle of taking some sort of inventory. "Let me introduce you to my husband," Mrs. Righteous said to the three guests. At this, the stout man looked up from what he was doing and looked at Prayerful's group.

"This is my husband, Scripture-Love," Mrs. Righteous stated.

"It is good to meet you," Scripture-Love declared in a deep, booming voice.

"Thank you. We are glad to have made it here," Prayerful replied. "I am Prayerful, and this is Steadfast and his wife Gentleness."

"We were just asking your wife about your town," Gentleness explained.

"I see," he replied. "What are you wanting to know?"

Steadfast questioned, "What kind of work for God is going on here?"

"Well, for one thing, some of the men are mining for the gold, silver, and precious stones of eternal treasure," Mrs. Righteous answered. "You can almost see the entrance of their cave outside this store. We also have large gardens that are constantly being cultivated and are producing the Fruit of the Spirit; and we even have teams of people who make it their mission to spread the seed of the Gospel throughout the world. Their goal is to lead people to the cross and start churches. And we also take a number of shorter trips in order to reach the people close by with the truth of our King."

Scripture-Love then piped up, "You will soon get to know Pastor Strong-Knees. He keeps everything organized and makes sure that everyone has spiritual food. You will also probably meet Mr. Soul Conscious before long since he is the one that organizes the mission teams." With a smile, he added, "That man lives and breathes the Gospel."

"We are certainly looking forward to meeting everyone here," Prayerful stated with a smile.

"By the way, we were also wondering," Steadfast said after a slight pause, "Could you help us find a place to stay?"

"Why, certainly!" Scripture-Love declared. "The person you need to see is Mrs. Loving.... She usually is the one that helps people with lodging around here."

Mrs. Righteous turned to her husband, saying, "Maybe I could take them over to her right now."

"Good idea," Scripture-Love replied. "Go ahead. I will take care of things here until you get back."

"Thank you," Gentleness said with a smile. "We certainly appreciate your help."

"You're welcome," Mrs. Righteous replied with a friendly smile. "I am glad we could help."

Prayerful decided to keep the purpose of his mission to himself for now. Though he figured that someone in this village would eventually be the recipient of the sword, he wanted time to get to know the people better, and he was hoping that the King, Himself, would make the answer obvious. Although he still had no idea as to who he would hand the sword over to, he was full of hope.

*   *   *

The days and weeks passed slowly for Prayerful. He was very eager to finish his mission, or at least to find the next step to take, but no matter how much he tried, he could not find any clear answer. In all of his travels, he did not expect a long wait once he reached his destination, and thus his former eagerness slowly grew into frustration.

During this time of waiting, Steadfast and Gentleness volunteered to go on one of the longer mission trips to the far out villages, spreading the

191

Gospel. They would be gone for a long time. When they had left, Prayerful felt even more lonely, for not only did he miss their companionship, but Prayerful also longed for Steadfast's wisdom and Gentleness's quite encouragement.

As he constantly searched for the one who could be the recipient of the sword, Prayerful did enjoy getting to know the people of the town. Over time, he grew to appreciate his neighbors, Humility and his wife Inward Joy, and he also grew to admire the wisdom found in men like Doctrinal Purity. There were many others as well who faithfully served the Lord, and thus there were a number of options for the recipient of the sword.

Prayerful figured that whoever was to receive the sword would be an individual who loves truth and has the courage to stand in the face of wickedness. He must be filled with wisdom and guided by the direction of the King Himself. Despite the variety of good prospects, however, Prayerful was still no closer to the answer than when he first entered the town. Although many seemed like they could fit the need, no one was just right — something was missing, and Prayerful was not content with any of these options.

Then, one morning, while sitting at the table in his house making breakfast, a thought occurred to him: *Wait a minute … I think I know someone who could carry the sword.* Prayerful could not contain himself at this newest idea, and he jumped up and began pacing back and forth. He had not been this excited since the day he had originally been given this mission.

As Prayerful thought about this man, he quickly realized that this individual seemed to be a perfect fit. In fact, *all* of the qualifications could be fulfilled in him, and Prayerful certainly would have no hesitation handing the sword over to such a man. The realization that he may have the answer to his mission sent a shiver up his spine.

While thinking on these things, a small voice seemed to whisper down from the mountain above, "Be not unwise, but understand what the will of the Lord is." These words hung in the air and caused Prayerful to go from complete excitement to bewilderment. Certainly, this man *could* be the right one, but was he? Prayerful was not sure how he could know for certain.

It was true that he may have found the answer, but he did not want to make a mistake in the King's business. Discouragement began to creep in at the silence from God, and Prayerful hung his head, feeling like he were back at the beginning of his journey by not having any answers.

Thinking back to the start of his trip, the words of Madam Wisdom once again echoed through his mind: "… In order to find the man, you must first know and understand the heart of the Lord, our King." Suddenly, it dawned on him that over the last few weeks, Prayerful had become so intent on finding the right man that he had forgotten the greater blessing of knowing God.

At this realization, the longing in his heart to spend time with the King awoke with a greater passion than ever before. He knew that, although he was just a simple man, he was allowed to speak to God face to face like a man speaks to his friend. How could he, as a lowly, weak, sinful man be loved by the King of Kings? How could he be allowed to draw so near to God that he would be able to hear the slightest whisper of his Lord?

With such thoughts whirling through his head, Prayerful knew that here, at Near-to-God Mountain, he *must* get to know the King! But how could he do this?

He already was at the end of the road, yet he knew there had to be something more. Not knowing what else to do, he got up from the table and hobbled over to the doorway. He needed to see Pastor Strong-Knees.

Prayerful limped his way along the street as fast as he could. He did not want to be rude to the people he passed by, but since his questions were urgent, he did not stop to talk. Pretty soon, he arrived at a one story, wooden dwelling.

Prayerful knocked on the door and was relieved when the Pastor, himself, answered with, "Good morning, Prayerful!"

"Hello, Pastor. Do you have a few minutes to talk? I have some questions for you."

"Certainly … come in," the pastor stated warmly. "Let's go into the front room where we can sit and talk." He led Prayerful into a small, but cozy, room where they both found comfortable chairs.

Right when Prayerful sat down, he began, "Did you ever know Passionate for Truth?"

"Yes, he was a friend of mine," the pastor replied, a little shocked at such a question.

"Well, I was there when he crossed the River of Death and entered the Celestial City." Pastor Strong-Knees raised his eyebrows in surprise, but Prayerful continued. "Right before he crossed, he handed his sword to a dear friend of mine and said that he was leaving his sword to the one who would pick it up and carry it into the battle for the King. My friend and I waited for months, but no one came to take the sword and carry on the work. Eventually, my friend was called across the river, and I was left alone with it. I continued waiting for someone to come, but no one did."

Prayerful paused for a moment, thinking carefully how to describe what happened next. "Several months ago, one of the King's messengers came to me. He told me that I was to find the man who would carry the sword and deliver it to him. The messenger never told me who this man was, nor where to find him. I had no idea where to even begin, so I sought council from Madam Wisdom. She instructed me to come to Near-to-God Mountain and told me that in order to find the right man, I needed to know the heart of our King."

"That was good advice," the pastor interjected.

"And that is my problem. I want to know the Lord more deeply, but the road that I was told to follow ends in this town … and I *still* don't know the King as I would like."

"The road does not end here," Pastor Strong-Knees declared. "It continues on, all the way up to the summit of Near-to-God Mountain. It only *seems* like there is no trail because there are so few who travel it."

"What?" Prayerful stammered, shocked at this information. "

"The road does not end here…. It goes on. You can always grow closer to the Lord, just like there are always more areas in which you can grow as a pilgrim. I have been up to the summit a number of times, and each precious trip helps me to know the King even better."

"Why haven't the people of this town told me about this?"

"Because a number of them have never gone up there," Pastor Strong-Knees explained. "I am constantly challenging everyone to travel to the summit, but there are those who still don't see it as important."

"Why?" Prayerful wondered.

"There are many reasons. For one thing, some are too busy to go." Seeing Prayerful's quizzical look, Pastor Strong-Knees explained, "Sometimes people can get so caught up in the activity of serving the King that they neglect their walk with God. Anyway, not only are some people too busy … but others think it is not necessary to go up there. They seem to believe that as long as they are faithful in their work, that nothing else matters. So, many are content where they are. They figure that if they work hard enough, they will earn God's favor … even as a Christian."

After a few moments of contemplation, Prayerful stated, "That's sad … to be so close to an intimate relationship with the King, yet be so far away."

"I know.… What is even worse is that there are a few Pilgrims who have criticized anyone who seeks to climb to the summit."

"Really?!" Prayerful said surprised.

"Yes. They claim that such people are either strange or have a 'holier-than-thou' attitude. These critics just don't realize what they are missing. Instead, they are the ones filled with pride. Going to the summit to meet with the King,… it is … well … unexplainable! I wish I could tell you what it is like to know and walk with Him, but it is too wonderful to describe."

Prayerful sat for a few moments, pondering what he had been told. "I want to go on up to the summit," he eventually stated. "Since Steadfast and Gentleness are not here, would you be my guide?"

"I can point you in the right direction, but this stage of your journey you must make by yourself. Your relationship with God is between you and Him alone."

Prayerful gazed out a nearby window, his heart racing with excitement at the opportunity before him. The purpose of his mission slowly faded into the background as the anticipation of a close meeting with the King intensified in Prayerful's heart and mind.

Onward, Upward

Prayerful, with the sword hanging at his side, stared at the sign in front of him as he steeled himself for this last leg of his journey. Just yesterday, he would not have imagined that he would ascend the slopes of Near-to-God Mountain itself, yet here he was, ready and eager to go. He took one last look at the sign, fully understanding its message:

The Way of Deep Love
*~And ye shall seek me, and find me, when ye shall
search for me with all your heart.~*

Glancing down the pathway, Prayerful found it very difficult to distinguish where the trail actually was. There was very little evidence of foot traffic through this area, only the flattened terrain where a road *should* go. Taking a deep breath, Prayerful began ascending the mountain path.

As he walked along with his slight limp, he noticed that the trail was not leading him directly up the slope, but rather it was taking him on a more gradual route around the mountain. He was thankful for this, for it would certainly be impossible to climb directly up to the summit, especially with his bad leg.

Gradually, the grassy road he had been traveling gave way to dirt and rock. Before long, it seemed like he was in a completely different world. He took a quick glance behind him and noticed that the Town of Faithful Christianity was completely out of sight; he was truly alone. He continued on for the next half hour, the silence only being broken by the clinking of his armor and the plod of his footsteps.

Knowing that the way could be dangerous, Prayerful had to work at being vigilant during this time of peaceful silence. As time wore on, however, he gradually let down his guard. It was then that it happened.

As Prayerful glanced up to the clear, blue sky, a terrifying roar pierced right through him. Instantly Prayerful's heart began to race as he spun around to his left just as a lion leapt from a ledge above, its outstretched claws heading straight for him. Instinctively, Prayerful braced his right foot behind him, and with trembling hands, he quickly lifted his shield to protect himself from this ferocious beast.

Time seemed to slow down as the paws of the lion drew closer and closer to him. The approaching lion was such a terrifying sight that it caused Prayerful to fear that he would not survive. Within moments, the creature crashed into the shield as Prayerful held on with all his might. At the moment of impact, the teeth of the lion clamped down upon the top of Prayerful's shield as the animal tried to rip it out of his hands. Prayerful pushed up against the lion with all of his might while simultaneously dropping on his right knee. The maneuver worked, and the beast was propelled over the top of Prayerful's head. Prayerful quickly caught his balance, and then spun about and stood with his shield in position. He was shocked that the lion had not knocked him to the ground with such an attack. *Wow! It's as if this shield seemed to take the brunt of the blow for me*, Prayerful thought.

In a flash, he had Passionate for Truth's sword drawn and ready to strike the terrifying beast. As his heart was pounding in his chest, he stared at the animal, not knowing when it would attack next. It was in these few moments that realization dawned on him: *This must be the infamous Roaring Lion!* Fear threatened to engulf him, and Prayerful had to work hard to remember the words, "Resist steadfast in the faith." He took a deep breath and steeled himself for the next assault. During these tense moments, another fear came to his mind: What if his knee gave out?

Without giving him any more time to think, the lion crouched and leapt at him once again. This time, Prayerful swiped at the animal with his sword while holding his shield in place and spinning to the right. Pain instantly shot through his knee, but, thankfully, Prayerful was able to hold his ground. Once again, the shield proved invaluable as the lion bounced off of it and landed a few yards away. As the beast recovered itself and got back up, Prayerful noticed a small gash in its shoulder where the sword had found its mark.

With pain shooting through his leg, Prayerful could tell that his left knee was ready to give out, and there was not much he could do about it; it was quite weak. Fear and despair began to sweep over him like a flood as he realized that he could not continue this fight. He wanted to run but knew that it would be both impossible and futile. At that instant, Prayerful recalled the words: "When I am weak, then am I strong." Remembering that he was wearing the King's armor brought a new hope to his trembling heart. It was not his might or power that would win this fight but the Spirit of God.

Shifting his mind off his knee and onto the King, Prayerful readied himself for the next attack. To his surprise, rather than leaping at him again, this time the lion crept closer and closer, remaining wary of the sword. When he was just outside of Prayerful's reach, he stopped for a few moments and seemed to study his prey. Then in an instant, the beast lunged forward and swiped at Prayerful's shield, trying to knock it out of the way. Once again, the shield remained un-moveable as the power of the King's armor deflected the blow for Prayerful.

Over the next few minutes, the lion attacked again and again, seeking to find a weakness in Prayerful's defenses; however, Prayerful stood his ground and let the armor of God be his protection. He also found that whenever he used the Sword of the Spirit, the razor sharp blade always found its mark.

With his confidence in the King growing, Prayerful cried aloud, "Deliver me, O Lord, from my enemies!"

As soon as he uttered these words, the lion opened its mouth wide and let out a loud and long roar, showing its terrifying teeth. The lion was clearly trying to intimidate him, but Prayerful refused to let fear dominate his actions as he locked eyes with the ferocious animal. He readied himself for another attack and watched as the lion slowly crept toward him, looking for an opening.

Just as the great beast was about to launch himself again at Prayerful, another nearby roar reverberated off of the mountainside. This noise was so great that the earth beneath Prayerful's feet began to tremble, and small stones came bouncing down from the slopes above. Strangely, though it was somewhat fearful sounding, Prayerful found comfort from this gigantic roar. He felt as if he had just heard the battle cry of an entire army coming to his rescue.

The Roaring Lion that had been crouching before him seemed to instantly lose all of its courage, and it began to inch away. Within seconds, this beast turned about and fled at full speed out of sight. Prayerful instantly knew what had happened: he had been saved by the Lion of the Tribe of Judah. Prayerful looked about, but saw no sign of his rescuer.

He sighed with relief and inspected his shield. There were no scratches or even indentations where his attacker had clamped his ferocious teeth down on it. Prayerful took a moment to breathe a prayer of thanks, for he knew that this victory came not because of his own strength or ability but because of the protection of the King.

Sheathing his sword, Prayerful took another deep breath and tried to calm his racing heart. Hobbling over to a nearby rock, he decided to take a little break and rest his knee. Much to his relief, the throbbing slowly diminished, and he was able to move his leg about more freely; it was sore, but manageable.

After taking a few minutes, he stood back up and turned his attention back to the path ahead, knowing that he had to keep his guard up. With his shield ever protecting him, he marched onward, up the trail.

As time wore on and the terror of the lion attack slowly faded into the background, he began to notice something in the distance that he figured might be an obstacle. Ahead, and to his left, a huge cliff stood like an impenetrable wall. He hoped that the trail would either wind around it or find a path through it, but at the present, he could not see any indication that this would happen.

After half an hour of traveling toward the cliff, his heart sank as he found that the trail suddenly veered slightly to the left and seemed to dead end at the base of this rock face. With a sigh, Prayerful walked up to the base of the cliff, discouraged at this abrupt stop. Knowing that he had not wandered off the roadway, his immediate thought was that he had to either climb or go around it. Looking to his left and then to his right, it appeared that this wall of rock continued on in both directions like a barrier surrounding the upper part of the mountain. Since the trail did not go to the left or right, Prayerful figured that the answer did not lie in going around.

Gazing up the smooth cliff face, Prayerful could not make out any way that it could be climbed. There were no ropes, ladders, or even footholds to ascend the forty-foot surface. The only thing he could see were the words "The Cliff of Busyness" etched into the rock above his head. He stood there for a few minutes, trying to imagine how he could get beyond this point. However, as no thoughts came to mind, he was at a loss of what to do and was even tempted to turn back.

Prayerful lowered his eyes to the ground and it was at that moment that he noticed something unusual. There, a small patch of lush, green grass seemed to thrive in the middle of this stony wilderness. At the far edge of this fertile ground, a small sign read, "And all things, whatsoever ye shall ask in prayer, believing, ye shall receive."

Although it seemed impossible, Prayerful instantly realized what he needed to do. He reached down to his belt and unloosed the leather bag that hung there. Opening the pouch, he took out the small box and lifted its lid, revealing the precious mustard seed of

Faith. He took this seed over to the middle of the grassy patch, dug a small hole, and buried it. He then bowed his head in prayer, convinced that something would happen, though he was not sure what.

After a minute in silent prayer, he suddenly felt something touch his hand. Startled, he jumped back, instinct telling him that some creature was about to bite his fingers. What he saw, however, was far from that. Right where he had planted the seed, a small plant was already stretching its leaves toward the sky, and, evidently, one of them had brushed against him. Prayerful gazed at the mustard plant as it grew an inch every second, amazed at how quickly it was shooting upward.

While he was standing there watching, he began to notice that the ground beneath his feet began to quiver. As the mustard plant stretched higher and higher, the tremor gradually grew into a full earthquake. Prayerful fell to the ground, somehow knowing this quake was the answer to his dilemma. He covered his head with his hands and curled up into a ball just in case some rocks fell from above — thankfully, none did.

Suddenly, Prayerful heard a gigantic *Crack,* and the tremors died away instantly. Looking up, he saw that straight ahead, the face of the Cliff of Busyness had split in two, exposing a hidden roadway through the rock face. In shock, Prayerful stared at it with his mouth gaped open.

After a few moments, he looked back at the mustard plant and had an idea. Not knowing when he would need the seed of Faith again, he got up and went over to the plant. He gazed at the fully grown mustard tree, and then grabbed a handful of the newly-formed pods. Once picked, they dried instantly in his hand, and he was able to rub them between his fingers, dropping the precious mustard seeds into his box.

When he had gathered enough and had the leather pouch strapped to his belt again, he took another deep breath and entered the narrow pathway through the cliff. As he trekked through this gorge, he soon noticed writing chiseled into the stone above. It read:

The Closet Door
~Enter into thy closet, and when thou hast shut thy door, pray to thy Father which is in secret.~

The climb through this narrow pass, though surprisingly smooth, was quite steep. It took a bit of effort, but Prayerful continued to press on. Sooner than he realized it, the walls of the gorge dropped suddenly away and he was standing on a level plateau. Straight in front of him, a waterfall plummeted from the rocks above and splashed into a large, beautiful pool. Looking ahead, Prayerful saw that the trail led straight through the pool and up the hill on the other side.

As he approached the water and gazed into the pool, Prayerful noticed that he could see his own reflection more clearly than he had ever seen it before. It was as if the water not only displayed his image perfectly, but also magnified it. Examining his reflection, he noticed various stains of sin all over him. Interestingly, it was only here in the Scripture Waters that he truly began to recognize the filth of his own sin.

While standing there, Prayerful was certain that he could hear the waterfall whispering, "If I regard iniquity in my heart, the Lord will not hear me." Although his sins had been forgiven at the cross, he needed daily cleansing in order to have fellowship with the King.

Prayerful bowed his head, confessed these sins,

and then waded into the pool. He found that, though the water stung his dirt-soiled skin, it truly was washing him clean. Despite the pricking pain, Prayerful held his breath and completely submerged himself in the pool — not one spot could remain.

After he finished, Prayerful waded out of the water and onto the far bank. There, he looked once more at his reflection and smiled with satisfaction. Not only was he completely clean, but he also noticed that his clothing was already beginning to dry.

Turning around to continue his trek up the hill, Prayerful saw another road split off to the left, heading back down the mountain. This was the infamous Way of Vain Repetitions. Although it certainly looked like an easy path to take, Prayerful kept his feet pointed in the right direction as he continued to ascend the steep slope of the Way of Deep Love.

On and on he climbed, continually getting closer to his goal. Eventually, he came to a place in the hillside that was littered with many carved rocks. Prayerful wandered over to the first one and was instantly caught up with the intricate detail of its artwork. The scene that he saw reminded him of all the things he needed to do once he got back home. Food needed to be prepared, plans needed to be made, and many other chores needed to be done around the house. Minutes ticked by as Prayerful subconsciously began to make a mental list of everything he needed to do through the rest of his day.

All of a sudden, he shook his head and tried to focus his mind. He knew that he should not stay here, but rather, he needed to keep going or else he would not get to meet with the King. Returning back to the trail, he continued on for several more yards when another stone off the trail grabbed his attention. As he stepped over to examine this one, his mind began to dwell on various memories from his journey with Believer. He remembered talking with his old friend and the various places they had been. He then began to think of how much he missed Believer and wished Believer could have assisted him with this journey.

After several minutes, Prayerful once again came to himself and said aloud, "What am I doing? I won't make it to the top if I keep this up." As he shook his head, trying to force his mind off of these memories, it all of a sudden dawned on him that he was on the Hill of Distracted Thoughts. He would have to take extra care not to go off the trail or else he might not make it to the top. Prayerful set his eyes on the summit and continued trudging along.

As he continued to climb, Prayerful found it was quite a battle to keep focused, and there were a number of times that he wandered off the path to examine various boulders, for each one was indeed a wonder to behold. He found that once he was off the trail, he would have quite a struggle to get going again. It took time, but he eventually discovered that whenever he wandered off the trail, he needed to *immediately* return or else he could be stuck there indefinitely, dwelling on things of the earth.

Thankfully, the further along he got, the easier it was for him to avoid the Boulders of Distraction. Keeping his eyes on the goal, he continued to take one step after another, and before he knew it, he reached the top of the hill. As he crested the ridge, a wave of peace washed over him, for before him lay a lush, green meadow with a single, large rock in its center. There was no higher ground to climb; this was the mountain's peak.

The Summit

Prayerful took a few moments to look around and was amazed that this small, green meadow existed like an island on the top of such a high and rocky mountain. Joy and excitement filled his heart as he limped over to the rock in the middle of the field. Not knowing exactly what to do next, Prayerful glanced at the boulder and saw one simple command etched into the stone: "Be still, and know that I am God."

Taking a few steps back, he pulled out Passionate for Truth's sword, sat down on the grass, and lay the weapon on the ground before him. He gazed blankly at it for a few moments, and then let his eyes rest on the hilt where the image of a cross and a crown drew his mind to the Savior. As he thought upon Calvary, Prayerful pulled out his Scripture roll from his travel bag. Opening it, he began to read the account of the crucifixion.

Reading the details of the sufferings of Christ and how He had been nailed to the cross made Prayerful's mind return to the time in his life when he had realized his own need for the forgiveness of Christ. He remembered feeling so empty on the inside; nothing satisfied. He also had been full of guilt over his pride, anger, and a slew of other things. It was when he was in this state of shame that Mr. Witness had faithfully pointed him to Christ. Though it was not easy, he had eventually heeded what Mr. Witness was saying and went to the Wicket Gate.

Prayerful could still clearly remember entering through this gate and traveling to Interpreter's house. It was there that this wise man revealed very important truths to him — such truths that he would never forget.

Prayerful lifted his eyes to the sky above as he thought upon what this wise man had shown him. The Interpreter had brought him outside where they saw a dehydrated, crippled man, desperately in need of water. Along came a noble man who saw the beggar's need and fetched a cool drink from a nearby well.   The cripple refused it, saying, "I can take care of myself."

The lame man took out his empty canteen and tried to drink from it, but to no avail. Then, he began digging in the dirt with his bare hands, hoping to delve deep enough to find a source of water. Eventually, he gave up on this and decided to suck on the freshly dug dirt, hoping that it would be moist enough to quench his thirst. This did not last long either.

Finally, after seeing his own attempts fail, he gave in and accepted the glass of water from the noble man.   Prayerful then remembered the words of Interpreter, "The same is true with men. Sin leaves us empty and full of guilt — after all, we are guilty before God. However, we try to fill our lives with all sorts of things that cannot satisfy the need in our heart. You see, our sin deserves the wrath and judgment of God, but God is rich in mercy toward us. He provided the way of forgiveness through the blood of Jesus. Only Christ can satisfy the emptiness and remove the guilt."

Interpreter had then taken him to the next room

where another beggar was trying to purchase a rare jewel. He initially offered the seller a worn out coat, but the merchant would not accept such a payment. Next, he offered the few pennies he had, but the seller refused by saying, "I will only accept ten thousand pieces of gold."

"The same is true with men," Interpreter explained. "All of our efforts to save ourselves are worthless. The blood of Christ is so precious that it is the only thing that can redeem a soul. Salvation from sin comes by grace through faith, not of yourself; it is the gift of God, not of your own works."

As Prayerful sat in the meadow on the top of Near-to-God Mountain, a peaceful smile came across his face as he remembered leaving Interpreter's house and traveling down the road. He could still clearly remember coming to the foot of the cross and kneeling with tears running down his face. "I am nothing but a sinner," he had prayed. "I am wicked … and unworthy. But I know you promised that if I call upon your name, I will be saved. Please forgive me, and save me from all my sin." Prayerful knew that he would never forget what had happened next, for the weight of his sin disappeared and was replaced with an overwhelming peace. While he had been standing there at the cross, he looked at the base of the hill and, seeing the empty tomb, he realized, *Christ triumphed over sin and even death — for me.*

As he was dwelling on these memories, staring off into the afternoon sky, Prayerful was struck with a different thought, *Only those who come to the cross and receive His forgiveness have the privilege of climbing Near-to-God Mountain.* He knew that the King would not allow anyone to have fellowship with Him without first being cleansed from sin.

Prayerful could contain himself no longer, his heart longing to speak to the King. Getting on his knees, he bowed his head, and began to pray, earnestly longing to meet with the one who saved his soul. He prayed for a while, and then remained still, listening to the silence.

As he was waiting there, a quiet, and yet warm voice filled with strength reached his ears. It declared, "My Sheep hear my voice, and I know them, and they follow me." Though he saw no one around him, Prayerful knew that the King was there.

Remaining on his knees and keeping his eyes lowered, Prayerful said, "My King, I am completely unworthy to even be here. I am just a wicked sinner."

"As far as the East is from the West, so far I have removed your transgressions from you," the King replied. "You were far off from me, but now you are made near by the blood of Christ. You have become a son of God because you have believed on my name."

"I don't know why you would do that for me," Prayerful declared. "There is no good thing in my sinful flesh.... I don't understand why you would die in my place."

"I have loved you with an everlasting love," the King replied.

As he heard these words, Prayerful's heart seemed like it was going to burst with joy and gratitude. He was awed at the goodness and greatness of the Lord, for no one could ever speak with such power and compassion.

"What I have already known about you is amazing, but your love and mercy are beyond my understanding. You are the Judge of all the earth and you do right ... and at the same time, you are so merciful and gracious. You are longsuffering and abundant in goodness and truth."

"Continue to grow in grace and in your knowledge of me. Seek to know *me* and walk with me every day."

"I will ... and I will pray to you, whether it is evening or morning ... or noon ... or any time of the day."

"If you love me, you will also keep my commandments, and they will not be grievous," the King said.

"I understand," Prayerful replied, "and I *do* want to continue serving you. You have always been so good and faithful to me. You have never led me astray."

"I will never leave you nor forsake you," the King promised.

Prayerful lowered his head as his heart filled with gratitude. "Thank you. My journey here has taught me a lot, and I long to continue and be faithful to you all of my life."

Being in the presence of the King was no small thing for Prayerful. Before he had come to the cross, he never would have imagined that such a thing were possible; in fact, he even had questioned the existence of the King. But now, things were completely different, and he longed to spend all day here. However, Prayerful knew that he still had to finish his mission for the Lord.

"My King, your messenger came to me and said that you wanted me to deliver Passionate for Truth's sword to the next one who is to carry it. I came here since I didn't know where to go to find the one you have chosen."

"It is required in stewards that a man be found faithful," the King replied. "You have done well in coming thus far, but my work for you is not yet finished."

Prayerful's heart leapt for joy at hearing these words, for he wanted to please the Lord and keep on serving. "Yes. And I will deliver the sword as you want me to. I have observed a number of people through my journey who I think could be well able to carry the sword; however, one of these men really stood out at me this morning. I had not thought of him before, but he is a man I have learned to greatly appreciate and respect. So, I was wondering, is Steadfast the man you have chosen?"

"I have not chosen him," the King replied.

Prayerful was a little taken aback at this, for he had been quite certain that Steadfast would be the right choice. After a few moments of stunned silence, Prayerful moved on to some of the other men he had thought of. "What about Pastor Strong-Knees?" he asked.

"I have not chosen him either."

"How about Meditation or Intercessor?" Prayerful continued.

"Neither have I chosen them. The Lord sees not as man sees; for man looks on the outward appearance, but the Lord looks on the heart."

Prayerful was a little dumfounded for a few moments. He did not know who else it could be, and he was out of ideas. Suddenly, another thought occurred to him, *Of course! I don't know everyone.... The sword is for someone else who I have not met yet.*

"Then who is the one to bear the sword? I will carry it to him and deliver it," Prayerful promised.

"Before I formed you in the belly, I knew you, and I have chosen *you* to bear the sword, Prayerful," the King declared.

Prayerful had to replay the words in his mind

several times as the realization of what the King was saying slowly sunk in. He did not know what to say for a few moments, being stunned and shocked — the King had chosen him!

"Me? ... But who am I?" Prayerful asked. "I am no one important."

"Certainly, I will be with you wherever you go," the King assured.

"But I am injured; surely someone else would be better," he stammered.

"My grace is sufficient for you, for my strength is made perfect in weakness. When you are weak, then you are strong. I have chosen the foolish things of this world to confound the wise; after all, I am the Lord, the God of all flesh; is there anything too hard for me?"

"Definitely not," Prayerful replied.

"The eyes of the Lord run to and fro throughout the whole earth, to shew himself strong in the behalf of them whose heart *is* perfect toward him. It is your heart I am looking for."

Prayerful did not know what to say and was overwhelmed at what the King was calling him to do. After a few moments, the King commanded, "Lift up your eyes and look out over the valleys below."

Prayerful stood up, walked over to the edge of the meadow, and gazed at the beautiful scenery before him. Rather than just beholding the hills, valleys, fields, and forests, like he normally would, Prayerful noticed the tiny towns and villages that speckled the landscape. He then saw that the valleys below were also filled with fortresses of the enemy. His mind instantly flashed back to some of the battles he had faced with Giant Flesh, Prayerlessness, and Covetous. He also thought of the havoc that was being brought about by the Enchanted Grounds, Vanity Fair, and the Fortress of

Lukewarmness. Having faced some of these enemies, he could only imagine the impact that these places of evil were having on Pilgrims.

"Ever since Believer crossed the river, you have had a growing burden because of the failure of so many Pilgrims. You saw the need as most of them tried to hold onto the world's goods while their eyes were heavy with sleep from the Enchanted Grounds. You secretly longed to do something about it and to see the cause of Christ advance. I put that desire in your heart because you have delighted in me."

Like the dawning of the morning sun, Prayerful began to realize how God had been preparing him all along for the task ahead. He stood speechless, overcome once again at the ways of the Lord.

The King continued, "The enemy has built many fortresses, and though some of my people have tried to assault them, they are still standing. Sadly, other castles have gone completely unchallenged. However, you need to remember that the weapons of our warfare are mighty to the pulling down of those strongholds.

"The problem here is twofold. First of all, many Pilgrims are content to live for the world and refuse to seek after me. They are willing to go through the motions but do not put me first in their lives. And then the second problem is that a number of those who do try to serve me are doing so in their strength alone. They have gotten off their knees and don't walk with me as they should. Remember, without me, you can do nothing.

"Also, because of all this carnality among so many Pilgrims, the gospel is not going forth as it ought. You need to understand that I am not willing that any man should perish, but that all should come to repentance. Although there are some who are still faithful, there is still much to be done.... The task is unfinished. Only when I call you home to the Celestial City will your job be completed. Until then, you must give your utmost to me."

Prayerful understood what the King was saying. Though many pilgrims were on the retreat, surrendering much ground, the Lord wanted all his children to be on the advance. The King was calling on him to take up the sword and push onward in the cause for Christ.

"If you go with me, I will go," Prayerful eventually said, surrendering to the call of the King. "But I will need help and strength."

"Remember," the King answered, "the Word of God is alive and powerful. The sword that you now carry is the same that all are called to bear. Others have important battles as well. Though various Pilgrims are called to different battles, all are to know me and to follow my direction as they serve. I will not leave you nor forsake you. You need to abide in me, walk with me daily, and *then* you can bear much fruit. It is not by might, nor by power, but by my Spirit."

Prayerful soaked in everything the King told him and continued speaking to the Lord for the next half-hour. Though he did not know what the future held for him, he was thankful that he knew the One who held the future. Through this time on the mountain top, Prayerful grew to love his King more and more. Consequently, he longed to give his all for God.

After their conversation was over, Prayerful knew that he had to return to his house for the night. He determined, however, to be in Scripture and prayer every day so that he could know the King even more. No matter where the service of the King would take him, he would always seek to spend time with God daily.

As the sun was lowering toward the western sky, Prayerful stood on the edge of the meadow once again, looking out at the land before him. The call was great, and he struggled with the uncertainty of the future; however, he knew that God would be with him every step of the way.

Prayerful slowly drew the sword out of its scabbard and held it in front of his face, taking several minutes to gaze at the hilt. The image of the cross and crown would always bear even greater significance to him, for he could never forget the meeting he had had with this King who died for him.

The ascent of faith must be done every day.
So no matter where you are along the way,
Keep your eyes on the goal,
And seek the one who saved your soul.